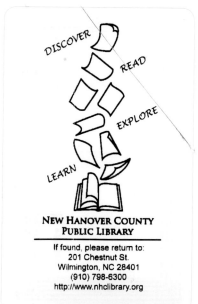

**NEW HANOVER COUNTY
PUBLIC LIBRARY**

this
impossible
light

this

impossible

light

a novel by **lily myers**

Philomel Books

PHILOMEL BOOKS
an imprint of Penguin Random House LLC
375 Hudson Street, New York, NY 10014

Copyright © 2017 by Lily Myers.

Library of Congress Cataloging-in-Publication Data is available upon request.

Printed in the United States of America.
ISBN 9780399173721
10 9 8 7 6 5 4 3 2 1

Edited by Liza Kaplan.
Design by Jennifer Chung.
Text set in Mrs Eaves OT.

To my mother, a woman of endless strength and love.

Unknown Variables:

An unknown is a variable in an equation which
has to be solved for. *Variable* comes from a Latin word,
vari bilis—with *vari(us)* meaning "various" and *-bilis*
meaning "-able"—meaning "capable of changing."

My Mother

is made of the bones of birds.
I look at her and hear the sound of twigs snapping.
Next to her I am giant
                clumsy
                obtuse.

She drifts through our house,
delicate wineglass in hand,
        filled pink and translucent.

Silver rings circle her knuckles;
Bangles clang together on her thin wrists.
She smiles at me
        a friendly ghost
when we pass each other on the stairs.

There's been more drifting
                more pink liquid
                less smiling
since my dad left three months ago.

Or

since she made him leave.

I don't have the story straight.
Don't want to know.

In this house we are planets in constant orbit,
tracing front door
        to kitchen
        to bedroom
        and back again.
Alone together,
a silent dance for two.

It feels like I haven't seen her in months.

The End

was sudden.
At least
it felt that way.

Like a balloon popping
        when you fill it with too much air.
    A vase slipping
        from your outstretched hand.

Everything was normal
until Mom and Dad walked into the kitchen
        one Sunday morning in June.

I remember
        Mom's eyes
        looking out the window,
        far away,
        at nothing in particular.

I remember
        Cheerios
        turning to mushy pulp in my mouth.

I remember
        Dad's voice
        sounding distant,
        forming words I'd never imagined hearing:

    It's just not working.

A statement that explained nothing.

I remember
        Mom
        crying
        saying nothing at all.

After the Shatter

it was something slower.

Her gradual pull

away

from me.

More far-off stares.

More wine.

More silence.

Tears hidden,

heard only

from behind her bedroom door.

Her skin thinner

translucent

her edges blending

into the air

around her.

And me

still solid
        left alone

on the shore.

Dad Moved

to a modern condo downtown
with one bedroom
    a view of the water.

       It's only a fifteen-minute drive, kiddo,
    he said

as if that were somehow
    close enough
to mean that nothing was changing.

It's been three months—
I've been to his apartment twice.
The second time he had a framed photo of his new girlfriend,
    redheaded
    round-faced
    smiling.

I don't go over there anymore.

Now
we get pizza sometimes
or see a movie
with my brother,
    Sky.

And we all pretend it's
    close enough
to how we used to be.

How We Used to Be:

A house wild
with mess and laughter.

Dad making soup on Sunday afternoons
in a huge pot on the stove
belting jazz standards as he stirred.
Mom painting in her studio.
Sky and I building pillow forts in the living room.

All of us driving every summer
to the Oregon Coast,
Sky and I speaking a secret language
       reading chapter books
       inventing games
in the backseat of the minivan.

Mom and I leaving each other notes
       going to the park
       driving to the waterfront
on the first warm day each year
     dipping our toes
     in summer's imminent approach.
My body curling into hers,
fitting so easily into the space
she made for me beside her.

A montage,
a golden family video,
a memory of someone else's life,
     the girl I used to be.

A girl I barely recognize.
A girl I envy,
a girl I mourn.

I Watch

the footage projected
behind my eyelids.

All of us around the coffee table
playing charades.
Me, seven or eight,
running excitedly around the living room.

Ivy's turn! Mom calls.

I skip to the couch,
pick a slip of paper from the bowl,
act out the title of *Alice in Wonderland*—
Mom guesses right away.

Good job, sweetie! she says,
her body clothed
in the same striped flannel pajamas
as mine.

I sit on her lap,
take a handful of popcorn,
growl at the opposing team,
Dad and Sky.

Try to keep my eyes open
as the evening dims;
wake on the stairs
as Mom carries me to bed
tucks me in.

Sweet dreams, Ivy.

Now I Know

the scenes weren't real.

How many
smiles did they force?

How many games
felt more like war?

When Sky and I were laughing
        in the backseat,
what was happening in the front?

How many
fights did they muffle
while I slept
oblivious and warm?

How many
years of tension rising
        pressure mounting
before it had nowhere
to go but
        up
        and
        out?

In Physical Science

last year
we learned about
plate tectonics.

      Giant pieces of land
      that move around hitting each other,
      grinding together,
      making volcanoes erupt.

I didn't realize
that families could
      shift
      erupt
too.

That we could be standing
on volatile ground
and never even
know.

When Dad Left

there was less of everything.

Like the house kept losing pieces of itself.

It lost furniture
      framed pictures
      the huge soup pot
      the old guitar that leaned against the couch.

It lost the fish-shaped waffle iron
we used to pour batter into
on Saturday mornings.

It lost my brother
      who got into cooking school
      and out of the house
as soon as he possibly could.

      I won't be that far away,
                    he said.
      It's close enough.

That's What People Say

about our age difference too

—*close enough*—

but

Sky got two parents
        together
singing
        painting
making soup
        and fish-shaped waffles
in the same house.

I was left with brokenness.
                The dregs.

Half a family,
together in silent orbit

                growing farther

                        and farther

                                apart.

Silence

has filled
the house
this long summer.

It crept in through the windows
                the cracks under the doors
so the space
      where the furniture used to be
is now filled with buzzing air
              and white noise.

I never knew silence
could take up a whole room:
      sitting on all the chairs,
      climbing up the stairway,
      thick in the air like fog.

Thank God

school starts
tomorrow.

Tenth grade.
        Finally.

Back to days neatly segmented
by classes
        worksheets
        papers
all lined up in my planner.

Back to bustling hallways
        shouts across the courtyard
        laughing during lunch.

Back to Smart Girl Ivy
        acing every test
        delivering her progress report each quarter
        with its sparkling 4.0.

I lay out my clothes for the first day:
soft gray sweater,
my best jeans.

Tomorrow I see Anna.
Tomorrow I start calculus.
Tomorrow I become myself again.

I've Always

loved math.
      The language of beautiful symbols
that whisper in neat rows
of patterns and exchanges.

I love
      the tiny even grid on graph paper
      boxing my answer in the right-hand margin.

I love that numbers never change.

Given two unknown variables
      and two equations
there is always
a solution.

Numbers never decide one day
they are

    just not working.

Whether people are laughing
      yelling
      silent
      leaving
2 + 2 will always be 4.
The quadratic equation always works.

Numbers keep their promises.

This Is What I Know:

Mom + Dad + Ivy + Sky = complete family

Mom + Ivy – Dad – Sky = quiet house
                                        less laughter
                                        no fish-shaped waffles
                                        so many questions.

Like how does
                    Mom + Dad
                    become
                    Mom – Dad?

How does addition
turn into subtraction
so easily?

Will less ever
feel like enough?

When I Don't Know What to Do

I count.

The world turns into

lists of numbers.

    Words and images get muddled

        like watercolors sloshing together

        into an ugly brown.

But numbers are clear and crisp;

they always tell a story.

    10: hours till school officially begins.

    6: classes I start tomorrow.

    3: more years of high school

    until I'm

    18: graduated,
        gone.

I Count

the raindrops
as they fall on the windowpane.

      Too anxious
      to sleep.

I stare at the corner of my street,
the occasional car's headlights
lighting up the houses
      as they pass.

My stomach flutters
      fingers trace the outline of my body,
so different
      bigger
than it was
just a few months ago.

Small lumps on my chest
      where there were none before.
More flesh around my hips.
Toes almost hanging off
the edge of my small bed.

This shape I make
hardly fits here
anymore.

Mom and I Went

to the mall last month
so I could try on new clothes
for school.

The store was crowded
so we shared a fitting room.
I faced the corner
   tried on a pair of form-fitting jeans,
so tight they would barely zip.

Mom's bony legs
        cut me from the mirror,
        yoga pants hanging
        off the sharp angles
        of her frame.

My hips full, round,
        refusing to fit.
My chest softer, flesh
beginning to push out
from under my shirt.

Felt hot
    sweaty
    nauseous.
Looked away fast
        pulled on a sweatshirt
didn't try on anything else
        all day.

We walked
        not talking
from
store to
store to
store to
store.

Paced the mall's shiny floors,
silent strangers.
I looked down at my reflection,
watched my silhouette expand.

This Summer

I grew
      two
           whole
                 inches.

Kept trying to ignore
      the too-short ankles on my jeans.

Soon you'll be six feet just like me and Dad, Sky said.

I don't want to be six feet.
I want to be compact
          able to curl up
          into small shapes
          like I used to.

I close my eyes
remember what it felt like
to be tiny,
      curled up,
      safe.

I Am Six

galloping into Mom's studio,
the converted garage
behind our house.

My small socked feet
slide on the smooth wood floor
        covered in pots of brushes
        and stacks of canvas.

Mom is painting.

        Who's that? I point.

It's Athena, she says.
The Greek goddess of wisdom and war.

I plop down next to her,
get out my watercolors.
        Mix them all together
        on butcher paper
as she tells me stories
about Athena,
how she fought Poseidon for the city of Athens,
        planted an olive tree
                        a symbol of peace
and won.

The air around us glimmers.
Mom conjures goddesses
until I fall asleep,
                softly,
in the light she casts.

Now I Stand

next to Mom,
feel how fragile
        she's become,
her shoulders,
her wrists.
Her flat chest
and narrow hips.

Imagine
that I can reach up,
press down on my head,
shrink myself back
        to how I used to be.

To someone small enough
        that I still felt
like her daughter.

Two Inches

in three months
is a continuous growth rate of = $\dfrac{0.667 \text{ inches}}{1 \text{ month}}$

If it continues,
I'll grow eight whole inches
in the next year,
      up
           and up
                  and up.

A girl giant
crashing my huge feet
over the city of Seattle.

That night
I dream I'm taller than the trees,
      expanding
like Alice in Wonderland
when she drinks the wrong potion.

I want to go home,
      she cries.
I'm just a little girl.

No one believes her.

I Wake

before my alarm.
Pull on my sweater and jeans
                a little tighter than
                when I bought them
                last month
pour a bowl of Cheerios.

Stack neat new notebooks
in my backpack,
each labeled with their subject.

Calculus gets green—
the best color.

Today
will
be
perfect.

Today
everything
starts
over.

I Take

the city bus to school,
                the shiny building three-and-a-half miles away.
The bus doors jump open
in front of me
with a snort.
I climb the stairs,
put in $1.50 in quarters.

My eyes flit back and forth
across the aisle
        adults on their way to work
        a man reading the newspaper
        a woman putting on mascara.
I touch my own face
wonder if I should have put
some makeup on.

Kids in raincoats and backpacks
sit with their phones in hands,
earbuds wedged into ears.
I put my own in,
scroll through my music,
click *Ella Fitzgerald*,
        let her voice fill the air around me.

Good jazz is like math:
a language built of rhythms
that take on a life of their own
        and become something
        with wings.

I close my eyes,
let the music carry me.

The Bus Stops

at the busy intersection
in front of school.

Kids
are
everywhere.

They cross the street in a blur of fishnet tights
                              zip-up sweatshirts
                              rain-slick backpacks
                              scuffed-up sneakers.

On the corner
a small circle of students
lean in to protect
their cigarette from the wind.
They light it,
pass it around.

One girl looks up
from underneath her blue hood,
holds my eye as I walk past
                like she's challenging me,
wondering why this pale tall girl
is staring at their smoke-ringed circle.
She looks inward again,
exhales smoke,
        laughs.

I push my earbuds in farther,
listen to Ella's voice
for half a song more.

Then
I'm looking up
at the big wooden doors,

kids on either side
of me
pushing in,
and I'm swept along
with the tide.

I Am a Smart Girl

which means

> I have a plan:
>> go to a top school
>>> study advanced calculus
>>>> organic chemistry
>>>>> learn how things work
>>>>>> graduate with honors
>>>>>>> become an engineer.

I am a Smart Girl,
which means

> I don't smoke cigarettes
>> I get all As
>>> I go to bed early
>>>> I exercise
>>>>> I make safe, responsible choices.

I am a Smart Girl,
which means

> I can't steal a bottle of my mom's wine
>> flunk a test on purpose
>>> stay up all night eating cereal and ice cream
>>>> run fast and far in the rain
>>>>> until there's no way back again.

But sometimes

> just sometimes

I wish
> I could.

It's Not

that I've been told *not* to do that stuff.

I just understand

> how I'm supposed to be—

> my place

> in the order of things.

Since I was little

people have always said:

> *Ivy, you're so smart.*

Now people say

> *Ivy, you're so smart*
> > *accomplished*
> > *impressive.*

When you're told enough times

the way that you are

it doesn't seem like

you're allowed to be

anything

else.

I See Anna

from a distance
before the bell rings for first period.
My chest warms
at the sight of my best friend.

Everything about her is familiar:
      the curls in her light blond hair
      her wild hand gestures when she talks
      her ever-present soccer bag.

She's been away in Paris all summer;
I haven't seen her since June.
She left the week after
      the distant looks
      the mushy Cheerios
      the *It's just not working.*

Great timing, world.

As I Get Closer

I notice
Anna looks different somehow
too.

She stands at her locker
        laughing
        with some girl wearing leggings and a pink sweatshirt
                some girl I don't know.

        Ivy!

Anna squeals and gives me a hug.

        Oh my god, how ARE you? It's sooooo good to see you!

Then before I can answer:
        This is Raquel.
        She was in the French program this summer too!
        You guys will loooove each other.

Anna is putting more syllables
                        more bounce
into every word.

The bell rings.

        Raquel and I have gym together now.
        Wanna meet us for lunch?

I nod.
Small smile.
They walk away.

And I realize
I didn't say a single word
the entire exchange.

In May

Anna said:
> *I'm gonna spend*
> *the whole summer*
> *in Paris with my mom.*
> > *I'm gonna take French classes!*
> *Isn't that awesome?*
> *Can you come?*

I begged my parents.
Both said they wanted to,
both said we couldn't afford it.

Divorces
> it turns out
aren't cheap.

So I traveled with Anna via pictures and posts—
> saw her body getting tanner
> > hair getting blonder
> unfamiliar faces smiling with her at the camera.
She looked
> so bright
lit up by sun.

I sat in the dark
at my computer screen
> tried to ignore that
just as she was
> reconnecting with family
> making new friends
I was losing both
of mine.

I'll miss you, she said.
> *We'll talk all the time. I promise.*
It was the first time
she's ever broken a promise to me.

Anna's Mom Left

when she was six.
It wasn't a decision
presented over breakfast.
It was yelling
        packed bags
        a one-way ticket.

Anna didn't see her for a year.
When her mom finally reached out
            with a new boyfriend
                    hefty bank account
                    desire to see her daughter
Anna left for Paris,
returning with stories of
        glamorous mom
        sparkling city.

Now she goes every year
for a week or two,
except this summer
her mom invited her for
        three
        whole
        months.

Anna wears her hair long just like her mom's,
saves up to buy the same Chanel perfume.

Paris has become
Anna's beacon,
her place of light.

A place she can escape to
        where moms are gorgeous and attentive to their daughters
        where life is magazine glossy
        where even broken families
        can still pretend
        to be shining and whole.

There's No Better Feeling

than the first class
    of the school year.

In first-period chemistry
    second-period art
    third-period Spanish

I line up my fresh syllabi
    in my three-ring binder
open each color-coded notebook
    to its blank first page
its lines impossibly straight.
    Everything still pristine.

I open my planner,
    copy down the week's assignments.

It's good
to be back.

At Lunch

I meet Anna by our lockers.
She's talking to Raquel,
        laughing.
Again.

Now I see
        what's different about her:
Anna is wearing a tight blue T-shirt
that accentuates a chest
she definitely didn't have before.

We used to cross our fingers and wish for boobs,
        worry that we'd never get them.

Now
I don't think I want them
anymore.

Now
I wear my loosest shirts
   wish to be small again.
                To go back to a time
before brokenness,
before long lonely summers.
Before so many good things
got up and left.

We Sit Outside

   eat our sandwiches
on the bleachers
by the brightly painted football field.

Me
Anna
Raquel:

not exactly the reunion
I'd hoped for.

They tell stories from Paris.
Anna giggles about a boy she met her last month there.
     Oh my god, Adrien . . .
     bites her lip and smiles.
     There was one night, at the beach . . .
       giggle
            giggle
       giggle
     I can't even describe it.

Her eyes light up
as she tells me
about sneaking sips of wine,
     the lights on the
     Eiffel Tower at night,
     the way Adrien's hands
        reached for her skin,
     how she'd wanted both
        to give in and
        to recoil.

My own skin begins to itch.

I listen to the music
of my best friend's voice,
  hear the familiar cadence
  but not the words.

Anna is back
        right next to me
but somehow it feels
like she's still miles

                                    away.

How We Used to Be, Part 2:

Walking home, arms linked, stopping to buy candy
every day after middle school.

Singing into kitchen spoons, all the words to the *Grease* soundtrack.

Making double-chocolate cookies that left the whole kitchen messy.

Lying on the hammock in Anna's backyard for hours
till we sunburned,
            throats dry from talking.

Doing cannonball competitions at the pool.

Scrounging up change to order a pizza, devouring it all.

Knowing how to make each other laugh.

Knowing what the other wanted most—
            Anna: Paris, first kiss, varsity soccer.
            Me: 4.0, new bike, all of Miles Davis on vinyl.

I kick the metal bleachers with my toe
   listen to Anna giggle.

If a girl
travels by plane
            at approximately 575 miles per hour
            for a distance of 4,994 miles
returns 3 months later
with a brand-new friend

how quickly will it take her
to replace
the things she left behind?

how long before the value
of what's familiar
shrinks to zero?

I Guess Anna

has gotten

everything on her list now.

She doesn't know that
mine has changed almost completely:
        parents back together
        Sky back home
        a best friend I recognize
        my body to stop growing

                        t
                        a
                        l
                        l
                        e
                        r

                BIGGER

              r   r
            o   e
            u   d
              n

Raquel Goes On

about some cute guy

from second period.

I stare

into my lunch bag

    remember the notes from Mom

    I'd find inside

back when I was little.

    Love you, Ivy

        or

    Have a great day at school, my smart girl

drawn-on flowers

    or a cartoon heart.

She'd leave notes

    on my pillow sometimes too,

a smiling crescent moon saying

    Sleep tight, sweetie!

They're still strewn

      around my room,

under the bed,

      stuffed in the desk drawers.

Littered artifacts,
the evidence
      of how we used to be.

I crumple up my empty lunch bag,
throw it in the trash.

Anna and Raquel

keep talking
    talking
    talking
when my phone
buzzes with a text from Dad:

    How is first day going?
    Want to get pizza tonight?

No.
I don't.

He always wants to talk
about the divorce
    my feelings
    his *concern*.

    Let me know how you're feeling,
he says,
and the back of my throat
swells and
my eyes burn and
I can't sit still and
I feel all itchy like
I need to get out of there.

All I can do is nod
    fake-smile
    look away.

Because
what do you say to someone

who doesn't live in your house anymore
    but *close enough*,
who you don't see every day anymore
    but *close enough*,

who doesn't love your mom anymore
   but instead
   another woman,
        round-cheeked and warm-eyed,
        smile breaking free from a frame on the desk,
   way
          too
               close.

I guess you don't say anything.

I pretend
I don't see the text,
throw the phone
back in my bag.

A Few Weeks

after Dad moved out,
  we took a walk through the deep ravine behind my house.

Summer spread itself around us:
  damp woods
  a winding gravel path
  panting joggers and dog-walkers
  warm light streaming through the leaves.

I walked in silence.

Dad tried to make small talk
but I was miles away.
Then he took a deep breath and said

You know, I've been wanting to talk about what happened.
With your mom and me.

I kept my eyes on the muddy gravel.

  I know what happened, I said.
  You gave up.

Stared at the ground
   straight ahead
    anywhere but at him.

It's not that simple, Iv—
  But I couldn't let him finish.
  My face got hot
  my brain was buzzing
  my fists clenched up.

  I have to go, I say. *Homework.*
Even though
it was the middle of
July.

Left him standing
like a mannequin,
awkward,
still.

I Got Home

and wished hard for Anna.
                  My best friend
who'd laugh
      and lay on my bed
            and braid my hair
                  and turn on a funny movie
                        and tell me it was all okay
we didn't need those
dumb adults anyway.

I emailed her right away.
She responded two days later.

Aww, Iv! That sounds so hard. I'm gonna call you tonight.

I looked at a map of time zones,
squiggly lines demarcating
      the world into stripes—
      Paris nine hours ahead.
I didn't know if she meant *her* tonight
      or *my* tonight
but it didn't matter anyway,
because she never called.

The Bell Rings

and Raquel skips off to fourth-period science.
Anna and I finally have a moment alone.
She side-hugs me and squeals.
 I'm so excited to hang out with you.

Finally.

Me too.

 I have soccer after school every day—wanna sleep over this weekend?

Sounds good.

We walk inside.

I take a breath
and let it out slowly;
 I have calculus next.

I Walk Into

the classroom and sit in the back,
the only sophomore
in a junior class.

One thing about being a Smart Girl
is sometimes you feel like
you're not supposed to be one.
Like you're supposed to say:
>   *Oh my god, that test was SO hard.*
Not:
>   *Actually I thought it was easy.*

The bell rings and I look up,
surprised to see
a young,
brightly dressed woman
in polka-dot tights
   short blond hair.

She introduces herself
—Ms. Fulton—
calls us *friends*.
Gives us a detailed syllabus
       an extra-credit worksheet.
I smile a full smile
for the first time today.

After School

the final bell rings
kids clear out of the hallways.

      I push out the big doors
        pass the soccer field,
      see Anna's blond ponytail bobbing
      as she runs.

Wave to her,
wait for her to see me
        and wave back.

After five minutes
I give up
walk the three-and-a-half
          miles home.

Mom's Not There

when I get back.

I check the living room
        her bedroom.
Nothing.

I let myself into her studio.

Canvases lean against the wall,
lie facedown in the corners.
Dried-up brushes tossed in haphazard piles.

My mother doesn't paint anymore.

But I still sneak back in here
        from time to time
to look at her dusty goddesses
smiling through their cobwebs:
        the jewelry
        of the forgotten.

She's Never Said

the word
>   *depression*
to me.
I've only heard her say
>   that word
once
>   when it slipped out
from under
>   her bedroom door
mid phone call
two months ago.

Later that night,
we sat silently at the dinner table.
She stirred a bowl of soup
over and over,
eyes on the swirling broth.

I asked her what was wrong
>   why she wasn't eating.
She stood and said
>   *My smart girl*
>   with a small smile
as if that was an answer.

When the door shut behind her
I sat there fuming.

>   If I'm so smart
>   why won't you tell me
>   what's going on?

Can I Tell You

a secret? she says.

Yes! I yell,
and put my finger to my lips.
It's the night before
my tenth birthday;
Mom is painting my nails.

She leans in.
I always wanted a girl.

I smile.

She braids my hair
while I blow on my bright turquoise nails.

She tells me about
growing up in Arizona,
how she'd play
in the dusty desert.

I tell her about my dreams
to be a famous scientist.

We know each other
by heart,
we tell each other
everything.

Now

every glance
every word
     is full of things
       she tries to hide.
Things she thinks
I can't see.

She protects herself
     with silence.

It's one of the many things
     I've learned
from her.

Compression:

1. The application of balanced inward ("pushing") forces to different points on a material or structure.

2. A transformation in which a figure grows smaller.

On the Second Day

of school
I don't see Anna before
first bell,
spend my free minutes
people-watching instead.

Boys in basketball shorts bump fists
        puffing out chests
        full of bravado.

Girls with stick-straight hair lean up against lockers
        chatting
        whispering
        texting.

I watch the girls
        who lean outward when they laugh,
        shoulders back,
        chins stuck out squarely
        beneath black-lined eyes.
        They congregate in groups,
        radiant
        thin
        in perfect-fitting designer jeans.

I stare too long
        catch myself
        look away.
Smooth my shirt
        over my waistband
        as I walk to class.

Chemistry

is a perfect beginning
   to the day.

We draw the periodic table,
   label each element with its

                           atomic number
                           mass
                           abbreviation.

I color-code mine:
   red for alkali metals,
   green for halogens,
   blue for noble gases.
Class flies by in a happy blur.

I picture myself as an electron,
   buoyant, buzzing down the hall.

After First Period

still buzzing
I stop
in the bathroom.

Two girls come in.
They talk loudly in the way that leaning-out girls do,
like they don't mind being heard.
Like they *expect* to be heard.

> *Your stomach is so flat! What are you doing?*
> *No carbs at all. I'm starving but it's awesome.*
> Giggle
> giggle
> *Oh my god, I'm so gonna try that.*
> Pause
> *After this cinnamon roll.*

They laugh again
        shoot glances into the mirror—
the kind of casual look someone gives
when they already know they look good.

I wash my hands

slowly,

study them.
The perfect fit of their jeans,
the absolute lack of frizz in their hair.
How can someone exercise that much control
over the way they look?
Or is it effortless?

They leave
without acknowledging me.

I stand there,
alone
with my reflection
        awkward
        frizzy

        inconsequential.

In the Mirror

all I see is plain
           plain
              plain.

Pale face, pale hair.
Eyes and lips unpainted.
Nothing like the faces
in movies or magazines.
Nothing like those senior girls
with their long lashes and thick straight manes.

I stare at my face,
         washed-out in fluorescent lighting.
I stare at my stomach,
      light pink, untoned
and wonder if I am missing out
on some secret—
        how to make my hair
               my skin
               my self
that perfect
that controlled.

I wonder if I could learn
how to do it
too.

That Night

I go into the kitchen
stare at the open fridge
        the half-bare cabinet,
try to pick something for dinner.

Mom's in her room
with the door shut.

        Wisps
of conversation
play on repeat
in my head:
        No carbs at all.
                It's awesome.

Nothing looks good.
I'll eat something later.

I head upstairs
finish all my calculus homework for the week
turn out the light by 10:00

and only then remember
I still haven't had dinner.

Strange
that I'm not even hungry.

I close my eyes
and dream.

A Month Before We Broke

there was a meteor shower.
The Eta Aquarids, Dad said.
He woke me up at midnight
to sit out on the roof,
    bundle in a blanket
and stare up at the sky.

At first,
nothing happened.
Then it lit up all around us.
Illuminated streaks,
        longer and brighter than the shooting stars I'd seen,
        crisscrossing above
        in the darkening night.

Dad was whooping
Mom was staring
Sky was grinning.
I was in the middle,
        enveloped in the night,
        the warmth and comfort
        of bodies on either side.
Safe on our roof
underneath a flaming sky.

Four weeks later
they told us they were separating.

I don't go out on the roof anymore.

In the Morning

Mom sits
sipping coffee
at the kitchen table.

I stare at her,
 wonder how long she knew.
  And why she didn't tell me.
  And if she feels
  like her life got trampled by
  a meteorite too.

She glances up
but only smiles
when she sees me looking.
Hums quietly
through thin lips.

I'M STILL HERE,
I want to yell.

Instead
I take small bites
of cereal.

Scientists Say

that telepathy is possible
between people who are *entangled*—
two people deeply intertwined.

They say
that two *entangled* atoms
      once connected
can still affect each other
from anywhere in the world.

I stare at Mom
in between bites
try to send messages
from my brain to hers:

> *Make me hot chocolate.*
> *Smooth my hair and listen to what I say.*
> *Remember what day it is.*
> *Remember when I have a doctor's appointment.*
> *Ask me if I have any homework.*

But she's looking at me
with an oblivious expression
      slight smile
      her arms so thin and breakable
      like they might snap
            if I hurl my words fast enough
      like she hasn't heard a thing.

I Knew Who

my mother was
when we painted together
        creating myths with brushstrokes
on the floor of her studio.

I knew who she was
when I sat beside her at her desk
        early in the morning
        as she worked on her computer.

I knew who she was
when she took me
to Green Lake
        every spring
to see the ducklings hatch.

Now

the studio sits unused
and the computer screen blinks on and off
and new ducklings hatch and grow each year
and I don't know her at all.

Smart Girl Goes to School

on day three
ready for her day of classes.
Listens to jazz standards the whole way there
floating on their waves of sound.

Smart Girl smiles mechanically
at people in the hallway
doesn't stop to talk.

Smart Girl hands in the week's math homework early.
Asks if there are more problems she can do.

> *You enjoy these, huh?*
> the teacher asks.

Yes,
I tell her.

I enjoy things I know I can figure out.

Finally It's Saturday

finally
my sleepover with Anna.
We can finally talk for real
like the best friends we are.
Best friends
        who cannonball off the diving board for hours
        who sing into wooden spoons like a whole arena is watching.

I get to Anna's at six
        eager to see the familiar rooms,
        the home away from home
                I've carved here
just like it always was.

We giggle about how gross
her younger brothers' room is,
watch *Legally Blonde*
for the zillionth time.
Laugh in all the same places
we used to.

Afterward I grab Anna's hairbrush,
sing the opening bars to *Wicked*.
We saw it together last year,
couldn't stop singing the soundtrack.

But Anna doesn't join in.
Instead she rolls her eyes,
sighs, and says,
                Oh, Ivy.

The Words Sting

hot and ugly.

Somehow
Anna has shifted
the tectonic plates beneath us.
We once stood on equal ground
but now she looks down from above
      observing me
        with eyebrow arched.

Oh, Ivy.

I put down the brush.

Anna Tells Me

things she learned in Paris
as we lie in the dark.

She learned

      if you dress in tight jeans

              a tank top

men will whistle as you pass

      a cigarette doesn't taste like much

but will leave you dizzy

if you exhale

      and look up at the sky

      a boy's mouth is

wet and searching

      both exciting and repulsive.

I wish I was still there,

she sighs

      like I'm not even here

and I wonder

if she ever returned at all.

On My Seventh Birthday

Anna gave me a heart-shaped box
     carved from dark wood,
closed with a tiny silver lock.

Inside were two necklaces,
     silver hearts dangling from each one
engraved with the word

    sister.

I lost mine when we were eleven.
     I finished swimming in the lake
to find its absence around my neck;
     couldn't find it anywhere.

I was scared to tell Anna
but when I did
she just shrugged.

    It's okay.
    You'll still be my sister forever.

My parents
     used that word too.
Now I know
    forever
doesn't mean much.

We Have Breakfast

with Anna's dad
            stepmom
            two younger brothers.

They laugh and yell
            Pass the orange juice
Where's the butter?
Anna tickles her brother
till he shrieks with laughter.
I look away.
     All I can hear is

            It's just not working

            Oh, Ivy

I make an excuse
leave before I'm done.

I walk home
scuffing my sneakers on the sidewalk
feeling the early-autumn air
            the unstoppable turning
of the seasons.

I wish I could
press some giant pause button.
Hold the good moments
            in my hand.

Wish I could crawl
inside my memories,
stay cocooned and safe.

Wish I could live
in the days of

        cannonballs
        pizza
        double-chocolate cookies
telling stories
with Mom
building pillow forts
with Sky.

I loved to lie under the blanket-roof
even after the whole thing collapsed
        waiting in my safe dark
for someone to find me.

Or I'd lie underneath
the dining room table and read,
        use the tablecloth as my shelter.
Watch the feet of my family walk past
        asking with mock concern:

        Where's Ivy? Have you seen Ivy?

I'd stifle my giggles
and just as I'd start to worry
that maybe they really never would find me
Mom would stick her head under the table.

        Found you!

I wouldn't fit underneath the table
anymore
unless I scrunched up my whole body.

Even if I could,
there would be no one
left to look for me.

No one to
even pretend.

After Anna's

I get home
find Mom in bed
      dozing
      with an open book next to her.
I close the door softly.

Wander from
room to room
      walk through thick silence.

I do all the new extra practice problems
Ms. Fulton gave me.
Quick.
Easy.

But no matter how many times
I try,
I can't solve for

      Ivy + Anna
      Mom + Dad.

There should be a clear answer,
something you can predict;
something unchanging.
No surprises.
Nobody becoming
      unreachable
      unrecognizable
      unknowable.

When I'm Done

Anna's sigh
    her voice
still ring loudly
in my head.

I need to get out of the house.

I slip on my sneakers
without knowing where I'm headed.
Take my old green bike
out of the garage,
yell to Mom *I'll be back later.*
Not sure if she hears.

I push on the pedals
  glide downhill,
relish how good
the forward movement feels,
the wind harsh on my face.

No direction.
    No agenda.
Just motion.
    Just pedal.

Pedal until thoughts
don't feel like thoughts
anymore.
Till it's just me
      the air
    the wild wind.

I revel in the push of my calves,
    straining up hills
      coasting back down.
The effort of my body
to get somewhere.

I bike as hard as I can
up the steepness of
Sixty-Fifth Street,
stopping only when I'm
completely out of breath.

I Set Down My Bike

panting
calves burning
cheeks stinging
feeling better than I have
in weeks.

Lake Washington glistens down below,
a shining blue jewel of peace.

My body
      feels strong
      alive
      capable of anything.

I look at the water,
      toy houses on the opposite shore,
tiny cars rushing past.

So many signs of life
all around
but
          no one knows
          I'm here.

I bike
      for another hour
up as many hills as I can
      to feel it again,
to keep feeling it:

      the power
      the control
      the push.

I Get Home

flushed
      feeling good.

Mom's lying on the couch
watching TV.

My stomach reminds me
it's been empty
since breakfast.
      Biking all afternoon
      I forgot to eat lunch.

Hey, Mom,
want me to make something for dinner?

      I'm not hungry, sweetie.

Fine.
I go to the kitchen,
look through all the drawers.
      Half-empty pasta boxes,
a twice-bitten apple
in the fridge.

Can we order a pizza?
      I yell to the living room.

      Sure, she yells back,
her voice
      a monotone.

I get her credit card
  order a large.

      Extra cheese.

Mom Doesn't Move

from the couch
    when the pizza arrives.

I take the steaming box
    into the kitchen
so hungry
and bite into the warm
    cheesy dough.

It sizzles
    fills my mouth and stomach
    with warm bread
        cheese and sauce.

I take a slice
    into the living room for Mom.

She's asleep
    empty wineglass in hand.
I put her slice on the table
    cover her in a blanket

go back to the kitchen
    and keep

        on

          eating.

I Don't Stop

        too warm

    cheesy

      filling

         delicious.

    Half
    is gone

      then two-thirds

    melted cheese

      hot red sauce

    thick crust

until

an empty box

stares back at me.

I Sit

next to Mom's sleeping body
on the couch.

She has always been
petite
but never quite so
         small-limbed
         bird-boned.

In clothes that used to fit
her body differently
      now I see
the sharpness of her collarbone,
      the protruding knobs of her wrists
      and ankles.

My hand rests
on my rounded stomach,

      so full it's
      painful.

      Feel nausea rise.

I Run Upstairs

        make it to the bathroom

lean over the toilet

pull back my hair

just in time

for the sauce

     and cheese

        and dough

          and spit

to force themselves out

of my throat.

Look down

      at the whole night's dinner

floating
    in toilet water.

I Shower

get in my pajamas,

clean,

no longer

stuffed

with food

and sleep.

I Wake Hungry

stomach producing
  a deep growl.
I feel weak
  still a little nauseous.
Run my hands
  over my belly
and feel
  how it's also
oh so slightly
  flatter
than usual.

I Get Dressed

pack my backpack.

     Pat my stomach again

before I head out the door.

Steal one more glance

in the mirror,

     smile

at my reflection.

Ready

     to tackle the day.

I'm Extra Focused

in my morning classes.
   Chemistry is easy,
Spanish is a breeze.

Smart Girl is calm and collected
   as the morning whizzes by.

I try to remember
to hold on to this feeling.

Anna and I

have lunch together.
I take small bites
stomach still feeling off
 drink lots of water
 listen to Anna's stories.
But
I'm so sick of
   Paris Paris Paris
   parties with her mom
   Adrien's perfect eyes
when she tells me
for the thousandth time.

Then

   Raquel's parents are out of town this weekend.
   She's having a party on Friday.
   Come with me,
she says.

I could make up a million excuses
    but the truth is
I just don't want to go.
The thought of standing
in the corner of someone's basement
trying to think of things to say
to people I barely know
   makes my skin itch.

The sandwich I'm chewing
turns to cardboard.

   I don't feel like it,
   I say.

She sighs.
Fine.

Anna never would have
cared about this party either.

Before.

Now she prattles on about
what she's going to wear
until her voice
becomes muffled in my ears.

I set down my cardboard
   stare at her.
         Can't we talk about the things we used to?
I want to say.

But there's no time in between her excited words
         or
I can't think how to start
         or
maybe I'm just afraid
her eyes will roll and—
Oh, Ivy.

How Can You Know

someone so well,
then suddenly feel like you don't?

We learned in chemistry last week
          that atoms get bonded together
but can be split apart
          without any warning
left alone to
          f
            l
               o
                 a
                   t
          through empty space,
unmoored.

          They didn't tell us
that could happen
          with people too.

In Fourth Period

Ms. Fulton puts a problem
on the board,

asks if anyone wants to come up
and solve it.
An integration with substitution.
        Tricky, but I can do it.

I look around the room.

Smart Girl has to gauge
        when the time is right
        when to raise her hand.
Wait
        1
2
        3

when no one else volunteers,
        I put my hand halfway up.

Ivy?

I walk up
        make my calculations,
box my answer.

Walk back to my seat,
        eyes on the floor.

When Class Ends

students zip up their backpacks
        bustle out.

I stand to leave.

     Ivy, can I talk to you for a second?

Ms. Fulton points to my
work on the board
    hands back my
      extra-credit problem set.

     You know, you're really good at this.

I smile.
I like math.

She smiles back.

     There's a statewide competition in January.
     They award college scholarships,
     and if you do well,
     you could advance to the national level.
     If you're interested . . .
     I'd love to nominate you
     to represent our school.

A math competition?
I didn't even know they had those.

I grin.
That sounds fun.

     Good.
     Here's the registration form—
     I printed it just in case.
     You need a teacher to sponsor you.
     I'd be happy to do it.

I take the form
        thank her
        grin all the way
        to fifth period
as little bursts of excitement
explode in my belly.

This Is

the first step.
     This is my plan
        falling into place.

After school
I am light
   happy
  free.

Unlock my bike
and
pedal
    pedal
       pedal
          pedal
home in record time.

Sky Got

a full scholarship
to cooking school,
an internship
at a fancy restaurant.

He's always known he wanted
to be a chef.

He had a plan.
He got out of here.

When I Get Home

I make a spreadsheet
of the top ten engineering programs
    in the country,
       their admissions requirements
           tuition
           research specialties
           location.

I print it out
tape it above my desk.

       If I follow a specific plan
       if I work hard enough
maybe I can get out of here
too.
       Build the foundation
       for Smart Girl's success.

That Night

Dad drops by

to pick up the mail

that's been waiting for him

  strewn by the doormat

  like litter.

Mom answers the door,

her mouth a straight line.

I watch from the top of the stairs.

They look at each other.

I look away.

Skin itches all over.

I go to my room

crawl under my comforter

read my spreadsheet

over and over

and over and

over

until it's all

I can see.

Dad Used to Come Home

at dinnertime most nights
        hang his hat on the hook
sit down at the table.

When I was small,
        I'd run and greet him.
He'd hug me and say,
        tell me the best thing that happened to you today.

Now he is a visitor.
        An unwanted guest
who won't cross the threshold.

A phantom
under the porch light
I can't bring myself
to speak to.

All Week Long

I breeze through my classes.
First history test
      first English essay
calc extra credit
done,
      done,
done.

I check off each assignment
      in my planner,
admiring each little box's tick.

On Friday
Anna asks me again:
      Come with me to Raquel's party tonight,
      please?

And maybe it's the way she stresses *ple-e-ease*
      or the familiarity of her smile
      or the realization that my alternative
      is another quiet night
      in a house with ghosts on the stairs
      and phantoms on the porch

because I hear myself saying
      Okay.

She claps her hands.
      Come over before and we can get ready together!

I smile in spite of myself.
Maybe this will be fun.

Anna Struts

in front of her mirror
that night,
putting on coat after coat
of black mascara.

Let me put some on you!

I don't know—

Ivy, come on. We're going to a party! You have to.

I bristle.
I don't have to do anything.

Whatever, fine, she says, and turns back to the mirror,
makes a kissy face,
turns slowly to inspect her outfit.

Ugh, I hate that my legs get so muscly from soccer,
she says, doing a 360 and staring at her jeans.
I wish my legs were long and skinny like yours.

Ugh, no, I'm way too tall, I say.
Then,
Okay, maybe just a tiny bit of mascara.

We Go Downstairs

and Anna boils water
for pasta.

*You have to eat something
so you don't get wasted,*
          she whispers to me.
*But not too much
so you'll still get drunk.*

          Um, I don't know if I'm gonna drink,
          I say.

She sighs,
takes a small pile of noodles,
          tilts her head and puts a few back.

Eat as much as you want, then,
she says,
walks away
into the living room.

          I stare at the pot.
Take a plate of pasta
follow her
sit on the opposite end of the couch.
The noodles feel heavy
          take too long to dissolve in my mouth.
I try to chew faster,
          swallow faster.

All right,
she says.
Let's go.

Anna's Dad Drives Us

to Raquel's.
Believes us
when we say it's her birthday party
           that her parents will be home
pulls away as soon as the door opens.

Raquel answers
wearing a strapless top
extra-tight jeans.
Her long tan arms wrap around Anna
               hug her tight.
     I'm so glad you came!
She looks at me.
     Hey, Ivy.

My excitement fades
like the slow hiss of a balloon.
     This was a bad idea.
     I don't belong here.
I want to grab Anna,
tell her this is a mistake,
that I never should have come
to a party like this.

But she pulls my arm behind her
and Raquel leads us to the basement
where a low beat is playing
     the cold air is wafting
       a small sea of teeming faces
          fills the drafty room
and I'm in.

A Group of Boys

play beer pong
on a table
in the middle.
Girls cluster around,
laughing.

Anna immediately joins them,
        hugging the girls
            exclaiming over outfits, hair.

My clothes feel all wrong
my body is awkward
                too large
                too full
and I can't think of anything to say.

I watch the animated faces,
hear the bustling collage of sound:
        laughter
        teasing
        the cracking open of cans

Either everyone else is having fun,
or they all know how to pretend.

Raquel Offers Me

a beer.
Anna looks at me with raised eyebrows.
        Um, sure, thanks, I say
accepting the cold can
        grateful for something to do.

Anna smiles at me,
lifts her can to mine.
        Cheers, to Ivy's first drink.

I crack it open
like I know exactly what I'm doing.

        See, I tell myself,
        I can pretend too.

The can is wet in my shivering hand.
I bring it up to my mouth
close my eyes
take a tiny taste.
It's sharp and tinny
like bitter fizzy water;
Anna's on her second
by the time I get just a few sips down.

I watch it all happen:
        the beer pong,
        the kids swaying
                to the bass,
        the girls flirting
                gossiping
        the minutes ticking by
        me
        wedged in a corner couch
        between two conversations.
There's nothing for me here.

I think I should go, I say to Anna.
She looks at me like I'm crazy.
    We've been here, like, twenty minutes.
There's an edge to her voice
that makes me stare back.
    She sighs, softens.
    Drink more, it'll make it fun.
    Trust me.
    I did it all summer.

But I can't force myself
to swallow the bitterness
any faster.

I Sit

and wonder
what everyone in this basement
is looking for,
if they are searching
      waiting
or if they really find this fun.

I feel like I'm in a play
and no one told me my lines.

No one's looking at me,
      but I know they can tell
I don't belong here.
      I'm out of place,
too big,
too quiet,

not a leaning-out girl.

Just tell me my lines,
I think.
Tell me my lines and I'll say them.

I Stay Close

to Anna and Raquel,
try to join their conversation.

They both talk louder
                    more excitedly
as the night goes on.

> *This party rocks,*
> says Anna.
> *And you look soooo great.*

Thanks,
says Raquel.
I'm so hungry. I ate, like, nothing today.
Beer has so many calories.

> *Really?* I ask.

Oh yeah. It's, like, pure carbs.

> *My mom is on a zero-carb diet,* Anna chimes in.
> *She's so thin.*

I feign only moderate interest,
look around the party.

When no one is looking,
I set down my almost-full beer
at the other end
of the table
                    far
away from me.

I Watch Anna

and Raquel start to dance
in the middle of the room.
          Other girls giggle and join in.

I stay where I am by the couch,
feeling full
watch them laugh
                    sway
                    drink.

I've always liked to watch people,
                    the particular ways
others dress
          talk
          eat.

Maybe that's the difference
between them
and me.
They are the dancers
          the centers of attention
          the subjects
I am an observer
          a study-er
          quiet.

I know no one will notice
          or ask me to stay.

So I creep up the stairs
          let myself out the front door
and walk the mile and a half
          home.

Alone

again.

I count.

> 22: blocks between Raquel's and home
> 17: seconds for the glowing red hand to turn green
> 36: kids crowding Raquel's basement
> 12: girls wearing tight skinny jeans
> 4: couples kissing in the basement corners
> 3: beers Anna drank before I left
> 2: shots of tequila Raquel took, laughing
> 1: shot I refused, its acrid smell turning my stomach
> 0: the number of times I bet Anna and Raquel
>   have noticed I'm gone

Sick of those girls
at the party
     so perfect
     so effortless.

Sick of myself
this body
that doesn't fit at parties
         or in mothers' arms.

Sick of this feeling
     trapped in this skin.

Oh, Ivy.

     Anna's sigh.

Pasta sitting like a block
in my stomach.

     Mom's tiny limbs.

Girls dancing in the center of the room.

Beer has so many calories.

My head spins.

I pick up

the pace

     count the entire walk home

let the whole world

fall away.

Half-Life:

For a substance decaying exponentially,
the amount of time it takes
for the substance to diminish by half.

Saturday Morning

I wake to raindrops sliding down the windowsill.
Their sound makes a safe cave around me.
I wrap myself deeper in my comforter,
   rub my hand across my stomach.

I don't want to get up.
The day is still perfect.
An uncracked egg.
Nothing has been ruined yet.

I hear the kitchen's bustling sounds:
        the dishwasher hum,
        the coffeemaker burble.

When you know someone so well,
you can recognize them
by the noises they make.
I used to know which
family member was climbing the stairs
just by the weight of their footfall.

Now it can only be one person
but still
        there's comfort in the sound of my mom
            out of bed
                    for a change
                brewing coffee
moving softly through the morning.

I Reach Over

for my phone,

    ready to return Anna's missed calls,

        to reply to a text asking where I went.

    I feel bad now
for leaving so suddenly.

The party wasn't terrible,
it just wasn't my thing.

Here in the early light,
it all feels washed away

    until

    I see my phone screen

      blank

    staring back at me.

Did she really
not even notice
not even care
that I left?

    She must've been relieved.
    No one standing between her and
    cool Raquel.

I turn over,
stare out the window.
Perfect morning shattered.

The Day

continues to tremble
and sprout fissures
as I watch my mom's hands shake
above the crossword she is doing.

Did you have breakfast?
I ask.

She doesn't answer
      sips her coffee
   just asks me
an eleven-letter word for *windfall*.

She looks so small,
her robe
too loose.

I sit across from her
at the kitchen table
look down at my own thigh
      mashed down wide
against the chair.

         Does she wish
         her daughter was made
         of the bones of birds too?

I don't reach for cereal
the way I normally do.

Don't want to stay here
with her quivering hands
      empty belly
      distraction.

As I leave the kitchen,
I hear her say,
Ah, of course,
inheritance.

It's a Sneaky Process

inheritance.

There are the good things:

    Mom's green eyes,
    Dad's love of jazz.

But there are other things too:

    the unspoken lessons
        that worm their way under my skin
        the things I wish I could unlearn

    the way it feels
    to watch Mom's thin wrists shake
    as they bring single almonds
    up to her mouth

    how I want both to steady her hands
        and also
    run far away

    how I want to see her full and happy
        and also
    look just like she does

    how I want to be nothing like her
        and also
    exactly the same.

I Grab My Helmet

and take my bike from the garage.

This time
I know where I'm headed.

My pedals take me
down Sixty-Fifth Street,
through the University District
to Sky's first-floor apartment
by the park.

I chain my bike outside,
catch my breath,
walk past the empty beer cans
and tattered couch on the porch,
knock on the door.

Sky answers after a few minutes,
        rubbing his eyes,
            yawning.
A grin breaks out
beneath his head of curls.

        Iv!

Hey,
I say.
*Uh, I was just
in the neighborhood, so—*

        he pulls me into a hug.

        Come in.

He Leads Me

through his messy living room
past
        furniture spitting its foam
        beer bottles
        cookbooks
        paperbacks
        torn flyers
        moth-bitten sweaters
        his roommates' bikes
        a drum set with broken sticks in the corner.

        Have you eaten? he asks.

Uh, no.

        Cool,
        he says.
        Leads me into the kitchen
        takes down knife
                plates
                cutting board.
        I was just about to make something.

I sit on a wooden chair
in the corner of his kitchen,
amidst all these wine-stained glasses,
        these signs of life,
let the warmth seep into me
despite the rain
continuing to drip
                drip
                        drip
on the pane.

Sky Cracks

six eggs into a pan,
heats hash browns
in the oven,

sets out
      coffee
      bagels
      cream cheese
      avocado
      tomato

hot sauce
salt
two plates
two mugs
two forks

sits down
and says,
      Dig in.

And I just do.

Hungry, Huh?

he asks
after I've devoured my second bagel,
relishing the thick avocado,
the tang of salt.

> *Yeah, I guess,* I say.
> *Thanks. That was so good.*

No problem.
I'm glad you stopped by.
I was gonna text you soon.

> *It's okay, I know you're busy.*

Yeah.
He rubs his eyes again.
I'm at the restaurant
six nights a week now.
But it's great.

Sky tells me about the internship,
          the noisy restaurant kitchen
          the mess
          the chaos.
He imitates the head chef
screaming about the *carrot juliennes too thin! too thin!*
I laugh so hard I hiccup
when I try to slurp my coffee.

So? What's up with you? he asks.

> *Nothing much,* I say
> licking the cream cheese
> from my fork.
> *Everything's fine.*

Because here
in this warm kitchen
with my brother
it really feels that way.

Sky and I

play two games of double solitaire
with old sticky cards
until he has to
get ready for work.

      Okay, I say,
      wishing I could stay
      just a bit longer.

You sure everything's all right?

I feel it catch in my throat:
a lump
of unsaid things.
Things like
      I wish you hadn't left
and
      The house is so quiet now
and
      What's wrong with Mom

but these things
can't find their way
to my tongue.
They get stuck
      change shape
      twist themselves into:

      Yeah, everything's okay.

The Rain Lets Up

as I bike slowly around the park,
    alone
    again
not ready to go home
just yet.

My stomach is full
from all the food
    that felt
    so good
    an hour ago
but now
sits like dead weight in my belly
    extending it
    stretching my skin
        tight.

Away from Sky's apartment,
it all comes rushing back.
    Mom's shaking hands
    Anna's radio silence
    the party last night
        these things
        that weigh me down.

My bike sags
with heaviness
    my jeans damp from the drizzle,
    waistband too snug,
    throat still stuck with a lump
    of things I couldn't find words for.

My body is full of things
that need a way out.

I imagine myself light:
moving with ease and grace
like airy sheets
dancing on a clothesline.

Imagine myself anything but
      solid
      round
      tired
      struggling
to push the pedals uphill
toward a house
that no longer feels
like home.

I Prop My Bike

outside the house
      sit on the porch
      watch the post-rain sky
wonder if Mom is
still sitting at the kitchen table
      or already back in bed.

My hand drifts to my stomach,
      the thick parts
      of my upper thighs,
      the soft flesh.

I think back to
the spread of food
covering Sky's kitchen table.

I feel sick.

Smart Girl

understands she is supposed to be
a certain way:
     good
     responsible
     careful
     strong
     healthy.

Now, sitting damp

         heavy

         tired

         full

I know

I am not these things

at all.

I Can't Sit Here

another minute
with just myself
     all my skin and softness

so I make sure no one is around
creep behind the bushes
in our backyard
kneel down
in the shelter of the leaves.

One hand holds my hair back,
the other reaches for my mouth.

Before I can stop myself
I stick my finger
down my throat,

try to empty myself
     erase
what I've done.

I Gag

and spit
comes out,
bitter saliva
     d
      r
       i
        p
         p
          i
           n
            g
from mouth
to dirt.

But no food.

I stick it in
farther—
     my finger
     my ally
     my weapon.

But it won't go far enough
so eventually I stop trying,
sit back
on the ground,

feel clean air float
in and out of my lungs.

The weight
sits stubbornly
in the cavern
of my stomach.

I Stand Up

brush myself off.

It's okay, I tell myself.
Just be better next time.
Tomorrow,
I have to do better.
Tomorrow,
I'll start being good.

Smart Girl
understands that hard things
require hard work.

I Head Inside

and up the stairs.
Mom's bedroom door is closed.

For the rest of the day
    she stays in her room
    the lump stays in my belly
    my phone stays silent.

I do my homework
  study my spreadsheet
  fill out the competition registration form.

Do ten push-ups
    fifteen sit-ups
before I go to bed.

Her door
doesn't open once.

The Next Day

I pour my usual bowl
    of Cheerios

eat half of it
remember
    my promise
    to myself
realize
I'm not even hungry.
      Throw
      the rest of the bowl away.

Soggy circles sit on top of trash
buoyed by coffee grounds
    banana peels
    remnants of other meals
      unfinished.

As the trash lid closes
a warmth seeps through me.

Today
I will be
    good
    responsible
    careful
    healthy.

So I do ten more push-ups
    fifteen sit-ups
    and bike and bike and bike,
      my body working smoothly
      as the gears themselves.

Monday Morning

Grab a handful of Cheerios
      backpack
      bike
take the long way to school.

I feel powerful
      capable
      buoyant

propelled through

first
      second
third
      period.

New strength glowing
      like coals in my stomach.

I do my in-class work,
      write down the week's assignments.
Raise my hand to answer chemistry questions.
      Capture the still-life fruit just right in art.
Get 100 percent on my Spanish vocab test.

      Smart Girl,
Strong Girl.

It's Almost Too Cold

to sit outside,
the early-fall air
nipping at our ankles

but there is still weak sun
so we sit on the bleachers at lunch

      Anna
      Raquel
      and me

and I give myself
two challenges.

Challenge 1:

Pretend to listen
as they discuss
      soccer potlucks
      the endless crushes
      who-kissed-who at Raquel's party.

Pretend it doesn't hurt
when Anna never asks
what happened,
was I okay.

Pretend I belong
next to them
when clearly
my input isn't needed.

Pretend to ignore
that they are pretending
too.

Challenge 2:
Tear smaller and smaller pieces
off my PB and J
chew them

as slowly
as I possibly
can.

In Calculus

I hand Ms. Fulton
my competition
registration form.

She smiles.
    I'm so glad you're doing this, Ivy.
Hands me a practice test.

Me too.
I smile back.
Thanks for choosing me.

    Back
on the right track.

I Get Home

that afternoon
see Mom sitting on the couch.
       My feet are tired, she says.
She looks at me
      asking with her eyes
      for something I'm not sure
      I can give her
like she is trying
to hold on to something.

I wish I knew how
she lost her hold
to begin with.

I draw water into the bath
pour in half a bottle of bubbles
till they float up into the air
like wishes.

We roll up our jeans, slip off socks,
pretend we're back on the coast
of togetherness and summer.

Sitting quietly
on the edge of the tub
it's hard to tell who's older.

I rub the tired balls of her feet,
feel the calluses accumulated
over quiet years.

Were you always like this? I want to ask.
Did I somehow never see it?
The words sink back inside of me
         get stuck
with all the other questions

I'm too afraid to ask
like

What parts of me are you?
and

When will you be better?
and

Am I turning into you—
          if so
how can I stop it?

How can I save us both?

We Dry Our Feet

change into pajamas
settle in the living room.

Mom pours a glass of wine
        pops a bag of popcorn
we huddle on the couch.

I curl up in the fetal position
   lay my head in the dip of her lap.

She strokes my hair
softly,
like she used to,
        eats a few kernels
        one at a time,
offers me the bowl.

It's so good to see her eat,
my own stomach starts to rumble.

One
two
three—
count the pieces as I go.
Savor my control from
hand to mouth.
        Satisfaction when I keep my hand
        still, when I say no.

Together we watch TV,
sharing what we can
through touch.

I Dig

for the words that swim
beneath my surface.

Hey, Mom—

But I'm not sure
          how to begin
          how to put words
          to what we've become.

          Mm?
She weaves my hair into thin braids.
I relax under
the familiar feel of her fingers
soft on my scalp.

Are you—are you okay?

Her fingers pause
resting still, light.

          Why do you ask?
          She is careful.

I'm careful too.
     Careful not to break this moment
               so precarious
               so precious.

I don't know . . .
Sometimes you just seem a little . . . out of it.

We dance around each other with our words,
skate on delicate ice.
Like if we say the wrong thing,
the other might break
beyond repair.

In my head
I dare her to say it.

To tell me
    what's wrong.

To tell me
    what it's like.

I want
    to help her
    to be here
    to listen.

I want
    her to stand up from the couch
    smile a real smile
    say
    nothing's wrong, don't be silly, I'm fine.

But she does none of those things.

All she says is
    Oh, I've just been tired.

And it's like every other time
when the bedroom door closes
behind her,
shutting
        me
              out.

The Weekend Comes

but I wish I could
stay at school.
Smart Girl doesn't want
          two days off
two days at home.

I work on a history paper
skip ahead to the next math unit
quiz myself on Spanish vocab
          then take my bike out
breathe in the solitude
               the cool air
feel my legs work hard.

I slow my pedaling
near the sprawling park
a block from school.

Little kids laugh
on the swing set
moms push from behind
          drink coffee from paper cups.

I walk my bike down the gravel path,
see their small bodies fly back and forth
through the autumn air.

I wish I were still one of them.
Back when life was so much easier
          when there was nothing to worry about.
Back when you didn't need a plan
                    didn't need to focus on the future.
Back when bodies were light and happy
          when families lived together
          when mothers took you to the park
on Saturday afternoons.

I wait until they've all gone home,
then hop on the swings
and push myself
      higher
             harder
above it all.

I Pedal

to a nearby coffee shop
to focus on the practice test.

Grab a table in the corner
pull it out;
drink in the numbers,
the sharp beautiful marks
on their white paper.

Go up
       to order a latte
       see the calories listed
              next to every item.

The bagels
     muffins
     croissants
so fluffy they
make my mouth water.

Everything looks so good.
Everything is so bad for me.

I turn away,
step out of line
without ordering a thing.

It's Like I've Started

some war within myself.

Just order the bagel.
       Are you kidding? It's a hunk of carbs!

It's not just Anna and me
that have split
like loose particles floating.

I've also split myself in two,
arguing voices that can't agree
that can't let me sit
in peace

so I abandon the test
get back on my bike
pedal fast down the street

but it's hard to get away from

yourself.

At Home

I finish the practice test,
score an 86.

Not
good
enough.

I need to qualify
        for nationals.
I need to win.

Need the scholarship
        the acceptance letter
            official and crisp
in my hands.

I know Mom
doesn't have much money.

I see it in her face
when she pores over bills,
heard it in her voice
when she couldn't send me
to Paris.

I don't know how divorces work
but I know they need lawyers
and lawyers cost money.

If I can do this right,
maybe I can help more than just myself,
maybe I can ease just one worry for her,
        help her be happy again.

Time to do what Smart Girls do,
and make everyone
proud of me.

I study
all
night
long
until my eyes are bleary
        my pencil point is dull
        I can no longer keep my head up.

On Monday

Mom texts me after school
asks if I'll pick up candy
on my way home.

I stare at my phone, confused
until I remember:
>   *Oh yeah. It's almost Halloween.*

Mom loves handing out candy
to the trick-or-treaters.
This thought makes me smile
so I pick up speed
pedal toward the supermarket.

Up and down the aisles
shiny under fluorescent lights
I pass the breads
>   cookies
>   doughnuts.

Suck in my stomach
turn my back on these foods.

Ignore the candy
Anna and I used to buy
>   Hershey bars
>   Kit Kats
>   Snickers

on our way home from school,
>   before I knew to read the calories,
>   before I realized numbers carry

their own weight.

I wrap my fingers around the smallest part of my wrist,
hurry to the next aisle.

But Each

golden baguette calls to me.
Each velvet brownie beckons me closer.

I want them.
I shouldn't have them.

My brain won't shut up
      won't stop arguing with itself
           back-and-forth-and-back-and-forth-and-back-
           and-forth
until my mind is a constant roar

and I can hear nothing, nothing else.

I hate this place.
This battleground.
This temptation.

                  I put my hands up like blinders
                      walk quickly past.

My Eyes Catch

on the bright purples and reds
of the candy bags
at the checkout counter,
        taste the sweetness
on my tongue.
The fruity gummy bears
the sour sugar crystals.

I grab a handful of bags at random
   shove crumpled dollars at the cashier.

Rush out of the store
back to the sidewalk

        sit on the nearest bench

        open a bag of sour gummy peaches

        stuff five into my mouth at once

        tell myself to stop

        then

        finish the whole bag

        and open another.

What Are You DOING?!

says a voice in my brain.
But I can't control
can't stop.
My hands move so quickly from bag to mouth,
bag
mouth
bag
mouth
and back again
and
my tongue laps up the sugary calories so fast,
I
am
powerless.

There is no pause button here.

Just my body,
acting on sinister impulse,
rebelling against me.

When I Finally

finish

I sit

among the wrappers,

feel

some dark fire

rising

in my stomach.

I need

to get

this out

of me.

I Bike Up

the steep hill toward home,

        body heavy with each push of the pedals.

Plastic bags
      empty of
      all the candy I devoured
catch the wind as they swing
      from my handlebars.

Everyone in
every car
is looking at me.

      My whole body inflates,

      bloated

      a balloon

      soft and weak

having failed

      once again

      to control myself.

This Time

      when I find some bushes

      in an alley up the hill from my house

      and kneel out of sight—

this time

I don't stop

when I start to gag.

This time

I keep going.

This time

I push

farther back

until it comes:

      the wrench

      the stomach flip

      the release.

Instant

welcome

relief.

>Reset

>the scale

>back to zero.

Try again

to be good.

When I Get Home

I tell Mom
I don't feel well
        that I'll get candy tomorrow
        that I just want to
        lie down and rest,
go right to bed.

I bunch my comforter all around me,
close my eyes tight.

        Hours later
I still can't sleep.

At 2:00 A.M. I get up
        stand naked
        in front of my full-length mirror.

Take an Expo marker.

Trace the lines
I want my body to make.

The glass does not respond.

Close my eyes,
see my outline shifting
to match this ink,
        transforming
        shrinking
        stomach pulling in
        legs whittling down.

Eyes open.
Memorize this new shape.

Step sideways out of my drawn-on reflection

go to bed

lie on my back

    feel the outline

    of my body

    terribly stubborn

    in its solid form.

In the Morning

I dig out the old bathroom scale

    from beneath the sink.

Set it down by the toilet,

    inhale,

step on.

    The number so much higher

    than the last time I did this, years ago.

But it's only

    a starting point.

    A gauge for my progress.

I memorize the digits.

A Fundamental Part

of calculus
are these things
called *functions*
based
on *input* and *output*.
Input equals x: whatever you're plugging in.
Output is your result.

The function is a machine,
an equation working its calculation
on anything you put inside of it.

If your function is $f(x) = 2x$
and x is 3
then $f(3) = 6$.

If your function is $f(x) = x - 4$
and x is 5
then $f(5) = 1$.

My body
is a function.

And I know
that the lower my x is
      the less I put inside of me
the better
my output
will be.

On Thursday

during calc

I make a list of the foods I've eaten today,

add their estimated calories.

It isn't until

six or seven heads turn around

               stare at me

that I realize Ms. Fulton has been saying my name

asking me to answer

the problem on the board.

My cheeks flush.

      Um. I don't know.

Her eyes linger on mine

for just a second.

I look down at my desk.

She calls on someone else.

After Class

Ms. Fulton passes by my desk,
hands me another practice test
for the statewide competition.

Is everything okay, Ivy? she asks.

Um, yeah,
I say
can't bring myself
to meet her eyes.

Okay, well, I'm always here to talk.

Thanks, I say,
stuff the paper in my backpack
leave as quickly as I can.

After School

I get on
my bike and ride.

If a girl
biking at 10 miles per hour
goes up and down a hill
at a 40-degree angle
7 times

how many calories will she burn?

How long does she have
to bike
until it's enough?

Exhausted

from biking,
I sit down with my science textbook
read about this thing called
a *positive feedback loop*.

Positive reinforcement of a system
leads to more positive reinforcement
speeding up the cycle
making it easier
       faster
       better
       better
       faster
       easier.

I take out the new practice test
  finish in record time.

The more I challenge myself
the harder I try
the better I get
the easier it becomes
      to be in control
      do all the right things
the better I feel
      the flatter my stomach
the easier it is
to continue.

When I get all the right answers
on a set of practice problems
I can
      bike in the morning
      study all afternoon
      do twenty push-ups
        thirty sit-ups

        eat a few bites for dinner
        finish tomorrow's science homework
        before bed
get up
and do it all
over again.

Every Day This Week

I play my usual game
at lunch—
see how long I can wait
between each bite,
how small the bites can be.

A lazy November rain
taps on the windowpanes,
lulls me into a mindless peace.

On Friday
Anna's voice
snaps me out
of my brief quiet.

   Ivy, how come you never
   eat your lunch anymore?

She fixes her blue gaze on me
and my stomach drops.
What are you talking about?

She makes a noise with her throat,
something laced with anger
and disgust.
   Like you don't know.

I don't,
I say,
eyes fixed on the unbitten apple
in my hand.

She makes the scoffing noise again.
Raquel shifts uncomfortably
and we sit in silence,
eyes averted,

the air between us
charged.

When I can't stand it anymore
I get up
throw my lunch bag away
stalk off down the hall
feel Anna's eyes
bore into me
the whole way.

My Mind Flits Back

to those girls in the bathroom
talking about flat stomachs.

Raquel not eating
before the party.

Every magazine cover
telling you how to
lose 10 pounds fast!

Anna cursing
her soccer-muscle legs.

Why is she mad at me
for doing the same things
everyone else
is doing?

For wanting the same things
everyone else
wants?

Maybe she's just jealous
that I'm actually
good at it.

I Stop

in the bathroom before class,
still feel Anna's eyes
piercing through me.

I stare in the mirror for several long minutes.
Examine each part of my body
like it exists on its own.
Like I can fix each one,
make myself perfect
            whole.

I wonder
        if my arms look thinner
        if my legs look leaner
        if anyone can see the progress I'm making.

And even though
part of me is still squirming
under Anna's anger,

another part of me
        a bigger part
is glad
she noticed.

That Evening

Dad asks if I want to get dinner.
I lie and say I'm not hungry,
suggest we take a walk instead.

It's easier to talk
side-by-side
instead of face-to-face.
I don't like the way he looks at me
so intently
like he's trying to see
what's going on in my head.

We amble along our block
in the cool evening air.

When I was little,
we'd take walks
and play a game:
Dad would point to a flower or tree,
I would guess its name.
  Rhododendron.
  Heather.
  St. John's wort.
If I got it right,
he'd give me a quarter.

I wish I could go back
to evening walks
that have nothing to do with burning calories
and everything to do
with the blooming greenery around us.

What's New?

he asks.

     Nothing, I say.

How's school going?

I dig my thumbnail
into the soft flesh of my palm.

     Fine.

I answer his questions on autopilot.
     Wonder if he can tell,
then realize I don't care.

He's only in my world
for an hour or two
every other week.
He doesn't get to know
what's really going on.

There is nothing I can do
except be quiet.

This silence,
     my only weapon.

I Keep Checking My Phone

to see if Anna
will text
    apologize
    make some joke
    remind me about our annual plans for *The Nutcracker*

       anything

that will erase what happened today.

I keep hearing
my phone buzz
as I'm about to fall asleep,
      but each time I look
at the screen
it only shows
the time.

She Doesn't Respond

to my texts over the weekend.

I can't find her

at lunch on Monday.

I sit alone on the stairwell,

don't even bother to take out my lunch bag.

When the bell rings for class

I see Anna coming inside with Raquel,

cheeks flushed from the cold,

both eating sandwiches from the café across the street.

I turn away

walk to calc

count the minutes until

the end of the day.

Class Drags

on and on.

There's a lump

in my stomach.

I copy down everything

Ms. Fulton writes on the board.

Numbers jumble together.

I mimic the movements of her pen.

Minutes tick by.

Finally,

> Remember to hand your homework in,

she says as the bell rings.

I reach for mine,

then see my empty folder.

> Wait—

I don't remember doing calc homework last night

> don't remember if I even checked my planner.

I stuff my folder back in my backpack,

walk out quickly

head down.

After School

I brace myself and stop by Ms. Fulton's room,

ask for another practice test.

I need to do better on these.

> She hands me one.
>
> *Okay, Ivy.*
>
> Pause.
>
> *I noticed you didn't turn in your homework today.*
> *Is everything okay?*

I just look at her.

I'm sorry. I know.
I need to do better.

When I Get Home

before I do anything else

I take the practice test.

    It takes me longer than usual.

    I score a 94.

Crumple it up.

    Still
    not good enough.

Write "100" in big red numbers on notebook paper

tape it above my desk.

            and up
         and up
Bike up

           the hills near my house.

Pedal farther
than I ever have before.

The wind roars,
blocking out all else.

When My Legs

are practically trembling
from the exertion
I head back home
climb the stairs
weigh myself.

Lower than before.

I smile
  hop into the shower
  massage my sore muscles

then climb into bed
and sleep
without dreaming.

When I Pass

a girl in the halls now,
it's like a reflex—
looking to see if she's thinner
or   w i d e r
than me.

Either way
it's a push forward,
a fiery breath of encouragement.

The skinny bodies say: *Keep going, you're almost there.*
The round bodies say: *This is what happens when you lose control.*

It's not hard
to pick which direction
to go in.

But Some Days

I'm so hungry
it's hard
not to buy something hot and filling
for lunch
  toasted bagels
  turkey sandwiches
  grilled cheese
  roast beef
and stuff it
in my mouth
all at once.

Some days I forget what book we're reading in English class

  some days I just want to fast-forward through the school day
      get outside and bike

some days I go through a whole pack of gum

  some days I watch the rain fall instead of taking notes

some days I glide through the hallways, barely aware I'm moving

some days I talk to no one at all

  some days I get home from school,

    head immediately to my room,

      curl up under the covers,

        and sleep till the sky is dark.

Some Nights

I look up at the moon,
trace its waxing and waning.

Each month
she gets thin and razor-sharp
before disappearing completely.

Some nights
I just want to stay in my cocoon,
where it is warm
where the moon's light shines down on me
where I can forget everything
except her iridescent glow.

I let it seep into my skin,
transmit its power into me
until I, too, become light—
        bright
        pure
        untouchable
shrink to a sharp point
then

gone.

Tonight

the moon is hard
to see,
clouded over by a muddy sky.

I lose
all track of time.

The alarm clock is my enemy,
        pulling me out of the deep fog of sleep
        into the even deeper one of being awake.

No matter how early I go to bed
I still wake up exhausted.

Once I'm up
I turn to the mirror
        examine each working part
        of my machinery.
        Flat stomach
        visible collarbone
        limbs long and lean.

Step on the scale.
The number blinks back
at me,
lower still.

Smile at my reflection
get ready for school
drink two cups of coffee in the morning
        one at lunch
that keep me going
all day long.

It's Funny—

I almost

can't remember

what I used to think about

      before this

what days felt like

      before they revolved around
         body
         food
         forward motion

I almost can't remember

    being excited to eat

    looking forward to dinner

    family seated around

      the dining room table

      over bowls of

      pasta and salad

I almost can't remember

    when calories were something

    I consumed thoughtlessly

not something to

      watch
      count
      cut.

Funny,
      this memory,
how it slips.

But It's Not Funny

when I sit down to do my calc homework

on Tuesday night

face my white paper

with is glorious sets of clean numbers

and can't concentrate

    can't find any notes from this unit

    can't figure out how to solve a single problem.

Not funny

when my stomach growls,

    head pangs,

    mind begins to count different numbers,

estimating and adding

the food I've ingested

today.

Not funny

when I put away my untouched paper

and stare instead at the

refrigerator door.

At least I still have enough willpower
not to open it.

Smart Girl

understands that
discipline is success.

The Wednesday Before Thanksgiving

equals the last day of school before
> a long weekend
> a few mornings of sleeping in
> days to bike fast and free.

Ivy?

Ms. Fulton calls my name after class.
I hang back,
she shuts the door.

I've noticed you've been slipping lately.

> All I want to do is
> get on my bike,
> go.

You haven't been paying attention in class.
You've missed a few homework assignments.

> My stomach rumbles
> loudly.

She looks at me straight on,
with kind eyes.
Mine start to feel warm,
> watery.

> *I know,*
> *I'm sorry,*
> *can I turn them in on Monday?*

I clench my fingernails into my wrist.
Carve crescent moons into skin.

Sure. Okay.

I turn to leave
but—

Have you been finding the practice tests helpful?
Do you feel ready for the competition?

I look at the ground.

      Don't know how to answer her questions.

We can run through some problems after school,
if you'd like. Monday?

I shrug.
      Okay.

Ivy, is everything okay? At home?

      I nod my head.
      Everything's fine.

She gives me a small smile.
Please let me know if you need to talk, okay?

      Thanks, I say,
already out the door.

I Almost Crash

into Anna,
standing outside Ms. Fulton's room
soccer bag slung over her shoulder.

Hey, she says. *Look.*
Exhales.
I'm sorry about before.
Sorry I haven't been at lunch.
I was just upset.
I'm worried about you.

I can't look at her.
          My eyes are still burning
and now everyone's talking at me
          with this concerned voice
like they think they know
                    anything about me
like they pity me
          all this worry, worry, worry.
I can't think
   can't take it
   don't need it.

          Worry about yourself, I say.
          She flinches.

          I turn
                    walk away.

After School

I jam in my earbuds

run outside to my bike

fumble with the lock

begin to ride.

I push and pedal

to the beat of Dave Brubeck.

I count along with the measures,

the complex 5/4 time signature.

With the rhythm pulsing,

the hiss of the ride cymbal,

the saxophone's winding croon,

the drizzle just beginning

to drop from the sky,

      the events of the day

      begin to fade.

I find my way

to some peace,

  a forgetting.

Wonder what it is

I'm thankful for this year.

Limits:

The values that functions or sequences approach as the inputs or indexes approach some value.

The Holidays

are a terrible time
if you're trying to avoid food.
Everywhere you turn there are
      pumpkin pies
      sugar cookies
      chocolate truffles
      mashed potatoes
      gravy
thick
heavy
filling.

I find myself
going in and out
   in and out
   in and out
   in and out
   in and out
of the bathroom,
checking my reflection constantly
tilting my head
      squinting
sucking in my stomach
gauging the fullness of my thighs.

Five minutes later,
go back in,
check again.

Sky and I

have Thanksgiving dinner
at Dad's.

> Dad kisses his new girlfriend,
>
> Naomi,
>
> on the cheek.
> I make a throwing-up motion
> behind his back.
> Sky laughs.

Naomi sits next to Dad
in a bright red sweater
   never-ending smile.
I feel sick.

> *Maybe he just wanted to be with someone*
> *who knows how to be happy.*

Suddenly
there's a lump in my throat
that has nothing to do with
the tiny bite of mashed potatoes
that's passed between my lips.

I excuse myself
go to the bathroom
spit it into a napkin.

Naomi's lipstick is on the counter.
Then suddenly
it's in the trash.

Oops.

As I Return

to the table,
Sky brings out
a pumpkin pie
he made just for
the occasion.

He sets it down,
            beaming.

I start to sweat.

He looks so proud
of the crust he spent hours
shaping
just so.

And he is my only ally
tonight.

He cuts slices
            one
            two
            three
            four.
Here you go, Iv,
he says.

Lift my fork slowly
take a bite
            to be polite
of smooth, warm pumpkin.

It is
so
SO
good.

One bite
becomes five
        six
        seven—
too many bites
and soon my plate
is empty.

Again
panic
begins to rise.

Again
my body
is not something
I can trust.

I Push My Chair

away from the table,
disgusted with myself.

> *Tomorrow, only water and fruit.*
> *Tomorrow I'll start being good.*

It's a promise
I make to myself
over and over again.

Sky Drives

me home.

We're both quiet in the car,
the radio talking for us
          punk music
low and fuzzy.

I stare at the other headlights
along the street,
let their rumble
lull me to almost-sleep.

          You okay, Iv?

I want to tell him
everything
but I can't.
He wouldn't get it—
he's a chef.
He eats whatever
he wants.

So I bring up
what is safe.

          Just stressed, I guess.
          I'm supposed to be competing in
          some math competition.

That's awesome. You're so good at math.
You'll kill it.

          Maybe.

Silence.

Don't you think it's weird? I ask.
Seeing Dad with his new girlfriend?

He exhales.
Yeah, it's very weird.
He's just . . . we're all just
trying to move on.

> *I don't want to move on,*
> I say.
> *I want everything to be how it was.*

I know, Iv.
But it's not really up to us.

I turn to the passenger-side window
so he won't see the t
                    e
                     a
                      r

sliding smoothly
down my cheek.

I Unbuckle

my seat belt
when we pull up
to the house,
but I don't get out
of the car.

We idle
   say nothing.

I look toward
the single light shining
in the upstairs window.

       Does Mom seem off to you? I ask.
       Like, not herself and really sad?

He scratches his scruffy chin, sighs.
Yeah, I think she's
having a hard time
right now.

This time I cry in earnest
         don't try to hide it.

Sky turns the car off.
It's okay.
She'll be okay.
Let's just be there for her.

Easy for him to say.
He gets to drive away.
I'm the one
who has to go inside
    push past the ghosts
       past her closed bedroom door.

Thanks for the ride, I say,
and get out.

All Weekend

I am good
        careful.
Water
        fruit
gum.

Mom and I
orbit each other
from
        room
        to
        room
        to
        room
like
silent dance partners.

I bike every day
        farther
                farther
                      farther

keep myself
in check.

I
am
strong.

Sunday Night

the hours creep by.

I sit at my desk

   face the calc homework

I didn't turn in last week.

        Smart Girls do their homework.

I take a deep breath.

        Now, start now.

But every time I look down

the numbers start to swim

and I keep losing my place

can't find the notes from this unit

    keep mixing up

        sine and cosine and tangent.

        C'mon, Ivy, this is basic stuff.

I'm so tired

        Snap out of it.

can't focus

        Do your homework.

so hungry

Don't deserve food—
homework first.

I wake in the morning,
pangs of hunger in my stomach,
with my head on my desk,
drool on my blank worksheet.

In Every Class

on Monday morning

I try to do

my math homework.

In every class

I can't concentrate.

I get through a few problems during lunch

      but I can't turn in

a half-done assignment.

      My gut is clenched and twisted

as I watch late-November clouds

swirl in a light-gray sky.

For the first time

since the school year began,

I'm dreading calc.

What will Ms. Fulton think

if I don't turn in homework

again?

Will she regret

nominating me for the

competition?

After lunch

    alone

    in the stairwell

    chewing and re-chewing a long stick of celery

I walk

    s   l   o   w   l   y

to math

until,

    one right turn

    away from the classroom,

I stop,

pivot,

turn the other way.

The Bell Rings

the hallways clear

my heart pounds.

I've never skipped

class before.

It's not something

Smart Girls do.

I could go anywhere.

No one would know.

I wander to the football field,

lie underneath the bleachers,

Sonny Rollins in my headphones.

For a second, I wish Anna was with me.

I look up

see the fourth-floor window of Ms. Fulton's class.

It's not too late.
I could go back.

But how can I go in there

when I'm not a Smart Girl anymore?

As I Lie There

under the bleachers
       freezing

I can feel it:

       the line

dividing

who I'm supposed to be,

       the girl I always thought

       I was

       slipping farther away

          out of reach

from who I am now.

I lie on my side,

damp grass pressing

into my cheek.

My stomach feels empty
          sick.

I close my eyes.

The Dream

is one
I know I've had
before.

I am sitting

in my living room

everyone is there

    Mom
    Dad
    Sky
    Anna.

Ms. Fulton is there too

and my grandpa Joe who died
    my godparents Sophie and Jack
    my first crush from sleepaway camp

only I can't remember any of their names.

I'm sitting on the carpet

in the middle of them all,

in the middle of their expectant smiles,

trying to remember

who they are

but their names won't form

in my mind.

I almost get the sounds

but then they drip out of me

like water,

lost.

I Stay

under the bleachers
despite the cold
through
     all of fifth
         sixth period too
flit in and out
of sleep.

I don't go

to Ms. Fulton's classroom

after school gets out either.

I bike around

and around

until it's too dark

to see the path,

go home

only when

all my fingers

have gone

numb.

The Next Day

Ms. Fulton stops me
        in the hall.

    Ivy, hi.
    What happened yesterday?
    I thought I saw you early in the day,
    but—

I look down.
I was sick.

Head straight to the bathroom,
check my reflection,
make sure
I look like someone
who knows what she's doing.

December Whirls By

under the constant cover
       of gray cloud
both inside my house
and out.

Each morning

I step on the scale

      as soon as

      I wake up.

Go to school,

stomach hardening

as I approach the place

I used to love

with a mounting sense

of dread.

Weigh myself again

      when I get home.

Watch the number fall.

Sleep,

      wake,

try again.

It Rains Here

almost every day;
a constant dampness,
the ongoing threat
of drizzle.

In our damp corner
of the country,
Mom strains her hungry fragile limbs
through the tops of evergreens
back to the dry heat of Arizona
the home she left behind.

She sits

in front of a light box,

a funny square machine

beaming out vitamin D.

It helps, she says.

Sometimes I sit next to her

as she soaks up the light

before I leave for school.

It's almost like

talking.

Close enough.

The Week

before winter break

Ms. Fulton hands back all

our recent homework.

I've missed so much

she hands me a note

  Please see me after class, Ivy

written in bright pink marker.

I fold the paper over

 pretend I don't see it

 walk quickly from the room.

Anna Stops Me

outside my locker.

Every year
since we were six,
        I've gone with her and her dad to see *The Nutcracker*.
We dress up
        drive downtown
                amidst white lights
                carols on the radio.

        The Nutcracker is on Saturday, if you still want to come.

I'd assumed I wasn't invited this year.

        Okay, I say. *Yeah. That'd be fun.*

'*Kay*, she says,
walks away,
blond hair bouncing
over her shoulder.

I watch her go
        and for a second
I really miss her.

She never turns around.

I spin on my own heel,
march in the opposite direction.

The Afternoon

is dark
>I move through the air like
>I am sinking in water

the failed history test I get back
in fifth period

>the paper with a big red C
>in English

my stomach knotting
face growing hot

>crumpling up the evidence
>shoving it in my backpack

biking home
as fast as I can
hot tears falling from my eyes

>longing for Mom
>to be home
>to hold me.

Her door's closed.
I knock.

No answer.

There is no one here
but me.

I Spend the First Day

of break
        wandering around
the house.

        Too much time
on my hands.
        Too much space
unoccupied.

I sit down in front of a make-up history test
my teacher gave me
before the end of class.
Read the same names and dates
over and over.

I go online to research
the Revolutionary War
        Britain and tea and taxes
but articles about how to get thin quick
        ads for diet pills
pop up by themselves.

I click and click and click
until I land on a blog called
Thinspiration.

Pictures
        of triumphant girls
in front of the mirror
        all sinew
        and success.
Their tips for conquering
        these bodies.
        Winning, each day, the battle with the mirror.
        They know what they're doing.

I search some more
bookmark all the best blogs.
     Check them throughout the day
     mesmerized.
A new rush
of determination
fills me.
     New strength.

If they can do it
so can I.

That Night

Anna's dad pulls up
in front of my house.
I slide on my coat
   head outside to meet them.

Christmas lights dot the neighbors' houses.
Ours is dark this year.

        Hi, I say as I climb in.
        Hey, Anna responds
        without looking up from her phone.

Her dad asks me about my family
and holiday plans.
I answer politely
until the questions stop.

The air is charged,
electric
in its silence.

Why'd she even
invite me?

'Cause you're still best friends,
says one voice in my head.
                Or 'cause her dad made her,
                a louder voice chimes in.

I cross my arms
stare out the window;
the lit-up boats floating on Lake Union,
white lights atop the Space Needle.
The same festive drive
we've made
for eight consecutive years

but this time

Anna doesn't want me here.

In Benaroya Hall

we find our seats.

Anna continues to text,
laughs at some conversation
I'm not a part of.

I don't know how I'll get through
two hours
of sitting next to her.

Then the room dims
     the curtain rises.
This is my favorite moment:
when the real world stops
and a new one begins.

The Dancers' Bodies

fill the stage,
moving their flesh and sinew in unison,
    legs
    backs
    arms
    taut and toned.
All strength and thin-limbed beauty.

I lose myself
in the perfection of their shape
   their human architecture.

Clench my abs
    on and off
    on and off
the whole show.

Afterward

Anna's dad offers
to take us for cupcakes and hot chocolate—
    another tradition.

Before I can reply
Anna snaps:
    Ivy doesn't want any, Dad.

My face grows warm
I look down
say nothing.

I don't know
what feels worse:

the fact
that she's speaking for me

or

that we both know
she's right.

Mom's Asleep

when I get home.
I feel the hunger
go to the kitchen
open the cabinets

      eat
      a single
      rice cake

close them again
head upstairs.

I find a note
on my pillow.

    My smart girl,

    Your progress report came!
    I didn't even need to open it. ☺
    I know things have been hard lately,
    and I don't tell you enough just how proud I am of you.
    Hope you had fun tonight with Anna.

    Love always,
    Mom

Another Pang

hits me,
sharp.

This time it isn't hunger.
It's guilt,
       sitting like sludge
       deep in my stomach
       making me feel
       fuller than ever.

I Can't Bring Myself

to open the report.

      My stomach turns,
      sick and full
           even though there's barely anything inside it.

Put Mom's note on my desk,
see the spreadsheet
of engineering programs
    my hopeful future
still taped above.
It's been months since
I looked at it.

I used to wish
I could take a break
from being a Smart Girl.

      I stuff the sealed envelope
      under my bed.

In the Morning

I take a deep breath
       open up my report
prepared for the worst.

     I see Ms. Fulton's loopy handwriting.

     *Ivy began the year quite strong, but she's now
     fallen rather behind, missed handing in numerous
     assignments, and fails to speak up in class. I'd
     love to see her catch up, but it will require hard
     work, and she has to want to do it.*

     More of the same
     from my other teachers.

I look at Mom's note
       her pride
       her smile
so rare these days.

     Shame
     is a hot, hot feeling
     a clenching of the gut.

I fold up the report
stick it back under my bed.

I Open My Backpack

look through
every notebook
   take out all the blank worksheets
          all the assignments
  I haven't turned in

       chemistry
       art
       Spanish
       calculus
       history
       English

It's all

too

much.

I crawl back

into bed.

When We Were Little

Sky and I would wake up before dawn
the week
leading up to Christmas.

      We'd cut paper snowflakes,
      spread frosting on Mom's sugar cookies.

We had lumpy knitted stockings
        on the mantel,
    a decorated tree
        sitting lopsided in the living room.

On Christmas morning,
we'd run into our parents' room
in our PJs
    beg them to get up
so we could open presents.

      Now I can't bring myself
      to get out of bed.

It's unthinkable
      that just a year ago
      I sat between Mom and Dad
      happy and oblivious.

Unthinkable
      that just a year ago
      we spent Christmas together
      as a family of four.

Unthinkable
how much can shatter
without our ever seeing it coming.

At 2:00 P.M.

I force myself
up and out.

Force myself to
       grab my bike
             feel the rush
             the push
             the control
       clear my head.

Force myself to put
aside the questions
that have been
fighting for space
in my brain

       like

Who is this girl
       who has trouble in school?

       Who avoids best friends?

       Who hides behind silence
              and distance?

If I'm not a straight-A student,
if Ivy + Anna no longer exists,
if there's no one I can talk to,

       then what?

When I Get Back

I hear Mom in the shower.

Look at myself in the mirror,
barely recognize who I see.

But
I know who I was
        who I used to be.

            Maybe I can still do this.
                        Redraw the line.

If I work really hard
        maybe I can do it all.

The Next Day

I spread all my papers around me

first thing in the morning.

Do some missed assignments for
             calculus
             English.

Then I check my blogs

        stare at the pictures

        of perfect bodies

        till they're all I can see.

Get on my bike.

Ride up and up and up.

Calves burn.

        Come home
        quiz myself on rules
             theorems
             equations
             formulas
do a
practice test
until my head spins.

Stop.
Check my work.

Get up and do jumping jacks

when my brain starts to cloud.

I can do this.

I Make

a new spreadsheet:
a practice schedule
counting down until
the competition.

> This is my chance
>   to redeem myself
>   to prove to everyone
> that I'm still Smart Girl Ivy.

T minus two weeks.

The Day Before Christmas

Mom asks
if I want to get a tree
but I can't see the point.

Why pretend?

Sky comes over Christmas morning
and we exchange gifts,
have coffee and hot chocolate.
He brings a homemade spiced bread with raisins.

I cut up my piece
take just one tiny bite
push the rest around my plate
tell him how good it is
so his feelings aren't hurt.

Then I sit on my hands
for the rest of the meal,
itching to get back to the work
waiting for me upstairs.

After We're Done

Mom says she needs to lie down
                          for a minute.

I watch her small body climb the stairs
to her room
one
    slow
        step
at a time.

Sky adds another log to the fire.

        She wasn't always like this, right?
        I ask when she's out of earshot.

He sighs, blows on the embers.

Never this bad.

        You're lucky, I say.
        I'm gonna get out of here
        as soon as I can.

It definitely helps, he says,
to have your own place and all.
But I'm still here, Iv.

I blink away tears
    turn toward the fireplace
    watch the flames dance.

The Next Few Days

all I do is

study
           bike
study
           bike
study
study
study
study
           bike
           bike
           bike.

T minus seven
        six
        five days.

Sharpening
           this mind again.
Strengthening
           this body.

I have never felt so
good.

On December Twenty-Ninth

Mom asks
if I want to go with her
to the New Year's party
at Sophie and Jack's.

I've got no plans of my own.
Can I get something new to wear for it? I ask.
I'm three-quarters of an inch taller
than I was in the fall;
everything is too short.

Sure, she says,
if it's not too much.

I browse online for dresses
        post-holiday clearance only
but my eyes gloss over the clothes themselves
focus instead on the figures wearing them
        hair curled gracefully around the chest
lips full and rosy
eyes perfectly lined
arms thin and delicate.

I click on *Intimates.*
See the same smooth-skinned,
bright-eyed, confident girls in their underwear,
        thighs tan and never touching
        stomachs flat
        skin like wax
        perfect bodies
        sculpted from marble
        staring at me
whispering:

        Can you make yourself into this?

I Can't Forget Them

for the rest of the day—

those perfect bodies

projected

on a constant, looping reel.

I break out in a cold sweat

remembering every Cheerio I ate this morning

      (fourteen)

and since I can't get them out of my head

I force them out of my body instead

      rush to the bathroom

      stand over the toilet's gaping mouth

      open my own

      let the Cheerios fight their way out

      in acidic triumph.

I'm Dizzy

when I straighten;

black dots cloud my vision.

I stand up slowly,

rest my hand against the wall.

Now
I am empty.

I step on the bathroom scale.

That can't be right.

Step off,

then on again.

The number doesn't change.

How

is it possible

that I'm no lighter

than before?

Each Time

I spit

sweat

gag

my body sheds a piece

of itself.

I imagine

cutting off the tips of my hair,

     filing down my fingernails,

          shaving the short hairs on my legs.

All these ways to whittle a body.

     I take off all my clothes

      step back on the scale.

     One pound lighter.

Just
keep
going.

Mom Knocks

on the bathroom door.

Ivy, are you okay?
I thought I heard you get sick.

> My breath catches.
> *I'm fine!*

Please go away, go away.

Okay, good.

I thought we could go to the mall.
You know, pick out a new outfit for New Year's.

> But I can't bear the thought
> > of trying on clothes
> > so I tell her it's okay,
> > I have something to wear
> > after all.

Spend the rest of the day
locked in my room
doing push-ups
        sit-ups
and practice set
after practice set
until I score 100
every time.

The clock strikes twelve.
I keep going.
T minus four.

I Decide to Wear

a faded blue sweater, jeans
to the party.
Old
     but comfortable.

I pick at my pilling sleeve,
sip apple cider by the fire.
Try to enjoy
the night away from
practice tests
numbers
equations
    T minus two.
make small talk with family friends.

Everyone keeps saying:
Wow, Ivy, you've gotten so tall.

Thanks for not letting me
forget it for a second,
world.

I Stare

at the dancing flames,

wonder

what Anna is doing tonight.

We haven't talked

in over two weeks

      since *The Nutcracker.*

I'm sure

she's at some cool party

with Raquel,

      drinking

      laughing

      dancing.

I'm sure

she's happy

she didn't have to invite me

this time.

I Eye

the decadent spread

on the dining room table

pick up a plate.

> Crackers
> cheese
> olives
> bread
> pot pie
> a whole roasted turkey
> all spread over green velvet cloth.

People mill about the table,

move food from plates to mouths

so seamlessly.

> Laugh as they scoop dip onto chips.

Chat with mouths full of buttered bread.

I throw away my still-clean plate.

Stronger

than everyone here.

I Watch Mom

from across the room
talking to Sophie
between long sips of wine.

Wrinkles frame the corners of her eyes
                                    and mouth.
She gives a smile so small
        I'm not sure if I imagine it.

When did I last see her
smile with her whole face?
I don't remember
what that looks like.

Sophie rubs Mom's back,
talks in a low voice.

I dig my fingernails into my wrist.

Mom never looks my way.

So I Get Up

and pour myself
some wine.

It tastes sharp, acidic,

      but makes my chest feel warm

and the edges of the room go fuzzy.

Mom looks over at me
      doesn't even acknowledge
      the wineglass in my hand.
I look directly at her, take a long sip.
      She only smiles weakly.

I get up and pour some more.

My Chest

gets warmer
     and the room gets softer

as I take longer, bigger sips.

I see why Anna likes this feeling.

I am loose,
     thoughts flood in
       funny and strange.
I tiptoe back toward the food.
     Nibble the circumference
of a cracker
     put it down.

     Get away,
     get away from the table.

I need some air.

The room swirls
when I stand,
     head directly for the door.

I Wander Out

to the deck
with five minutes until midnight.
It's chilly out
but my insides feel warm.
       Take my socks off,
bare feet cold against the wood.

The sky is clear tonight,
       the moon almost full.
The tops of evergreens tower above the house.
Breeze dances through my hair.

Anna and I
used to write
New Year's resolutions
together every year,
read them out loud
just before twelve:

       finally jump off the high dive
or
       get my learner's permit
or
       have my first kiss.

I wonder what
hers are this year.

The countdown starts
       inside.

Happy, drunken voices shout:
       Ten! Nine! Eight!

This year I keep
my resolutions to myself:

      1. Win the competition, get a scholarship.
      2. Make my body flawless.

The First Day

of the new year
is a rush of preparation.

      T minus one.

I wake early,
head aching.

Gulp water,
rub my temples,
try to focus
      bright and sharp
      laser-like
on the practice test
      in front of me.

T minus twenty hours

      sixteen

      ten.

After each round
I bike.

I am a machine.

I train myself
      to perfection.

The Night Before

the competition
I can't sleep.

Hunger gnaws at me.

The moon is waning now,
      a disappearing Cheshire cat smile.

I check my alarm again and again.

Each time I slip into sleep
it feels like I'm falling
and I wake with a start
         sweating
worried I've missed it completely.

My blankets twist around my ankles.
I turn my pillow over and over,
      try to cool down.

It feels like I'm awake
all night
  but then suddenly
    my alarm is blaring
and I'm pulled out
  of a dream
      dragging myself up
        once more.

6:30 A.M.

Everything is
    planned
    precise
    ready.

My tired body glides from
                toothbrush
                to sweater
                to backpack
every movement smooth
            and exact.

I boil water for coffee,
lay out ten almonds in a straight line

eat them one by one.

Today

I

will

be

perfect.

I Get on My Bike

and launch forward,
backpack pressing down
        against my shoulders,
legs firm on the pedals.

The sky is brightening all around me—
no one else outside,
just the sound of birdcalls
    the wind against my face
        gravel crunching beneath my tires.

In these early-morning hours
I am the only one alive.

I Lean Forward

cruising faster,
taking smooth turns
at each corner.

I see myself
from a bird's-eye view,
making precise geometric shapes
as I zoom from street
to perpendicular street.

Swift wind blows past my cheeks.
I am weightless
     light
     dizzy with excitement
propelling forward and
                 forward and
                          forward
body in sync with the effortless gears on my bike
the world around me a roaring blur of color.

I am pushing
I am flying
I am air
I am light
     light-headed

I am swirling

            swerving

I am losing

            my vision

I

see black

dots I

see

nothing

So Many

things must happen
      correctly
for the body
      to function

so many muscles
      tendons
      ligaments
      neurons
      nerves
must cooperate.

Lying
beneath my bike
      my arm
      twisted under me
      at an angle
      it has never made
      before
my body
      is not working
at all.

It takes several seconds
for the pain
to hit

and when it does
I turn over
and puke.

I Can't

get up.
My head spins.
Everything aches.
My arm is made of needles,
hot
hot.

Help,
I yell
or whisper.

Can't tell if my voice
is working,
can't tell where I am
   or if anyone
can see me.

I taste blood
almond
acid.

Lay my head down
in a pool of bile.

HEY!

A voice screams.
Feet pound toward me.

Oh my god, are you okay?

The feet pound closer.
The voice speaks into a phone.
Loud, loud music plays.

Eventually,
men lift me.

I close my eyes.

Discontinuous Function:

A discontinuity is the point at which a mathematical object
is discontinuous.
If there is a break in the function of any kind,
then it is discontinuous.
Discontinuous/discontinuity is defined as a distinct break
in physical continuity or sequence in time.

A Gash

in the forehead,
blood where I bit
my tongue.

Bruising and scrapes
on the left side of my body

the left arm broken
in two places
where it shot out
to protect me.

Quite a fall,
says the doctor in the ER,
but it will heal.

He's putting the cast on
when Mom comes rushing in.

    Oh, honey.

She hugs me
and I wince.

I'm fine,
I say.
    A reflex.

This time
we both know
it isn't true.

I Grit

my teeth as the doctor
sews three small stitches
across my forehead.

Dad walks in.
                    Ivy!

Please go away, go away.

What hurts worse
than the punctures in my head
        my broken arm
        the bruises up my side
is the sight
of both my parents
in front of me:

Dad on my left
        grabbing my hand
Mom on my right
        smoothing my hair.

How can they bear to talk to each other
                        to exist in the same space
        after ripping apart something
        that was supposed to stay whole?

How can they stand there
without bleeding,
bleeding?

Thankfully

the doctor disrupts this
        messed-up Hallmark moment

            puts a bandage on me
and turns to them.

Mr. and Mrs. Lewis?
Can I talk to you outside?

            That's not their name anymore,
            I say.

They leave,
and I'm
alone.

I Watch the Clock

each terrible tick
of the second hand
taking me farther
from where
I need to be:

the school hosting the competition
full of lined-up desks
        sharpened pencils
        derivatives
        my chance
                at redemption.

T minus ten minutes.

Time is
running
out.

Some Scientists Believe

we live in a multiverse
full of parallel lives.

In a parallel universe
I never fell off my bike.

I am sitting at my assigned desk
with two sharpened pencils
    smiling
      answering the last problem
       correctly.

I set down my pencil
  close my test booklet
  hand it to the proctor.

I am the first one
finished.

I receive a letter
of congratulations
weeks from now,
    awarding me
the college scholarship

      the scholarship that will make
      everyone beam with pride

      the scholarship that will take
      me out of here.

In a parallel universe
my family is still whole
my body is unbroken.

But I don't believe in
the multiverse.

When My Parents Come Back

it's all furrowed brows
      wide eyes
      soft voices.

A new doctor is with them.

They approach me
like I'm glass.

> *Hi, Ivy, I'm Dr. Marshall.*

> *There are a few things*
> *we'd like to talk*
> *to you about.*

She says it slowly
like I'm too dumb
to understand.

> *Can I ask you some questions?*

I look at my parents,
      then away just as quickly.

Open my mouth
but nothing comes out.

Dr. Marshall hears
what I can't say
and asks them
to leave the room.

The Questions Dr. Marshall Asks

are ones I can't answer.

Do you ever or have you ever restricted your diet?
Do you ever or have you ever purposely thrown up after eating?

I don't know what to say.
I am used to getting the answers right
but there are no right answers here.

Each question is
          an accusation
a sharp arrow in my side.

I feel like I've done something terribly wrong
when all along
I've just been trying
to be good.

The Words She Uses

include ones I know,
like:

> *body mass index*
> *high stress*
> *fatigue*
> *overexertion*

but there are also ones I don't,
like:

> *disordered eating*
> *body dysmorphia*
> *possible dysthymia*
> *low hemoglobin.*

She says
my perfect machine
isn't working right

she says
the function of my body
is flawed

she says
I may have done
some serious damage

but all I hear is
> the blood surging through
> my ears,
> echoing
> *I'm fine*

> the ticking of the clock
> telling me it's
> far
> too late.

Dad Leaves the Hospital

with a hug and a promise
        to check on me tomorrow.

Mom drives me home.
Together
we are silent.

        I nestle my bright-blue cast
on my lap,
        lean my head
against the passenger-side window
as we come to
a red light.

        Where were you biking so early, Iv?
        she asks.

I sigh.

Nowhere important.

It's Noon

by the time
we get home.

The competition
is over.

Everything
hurts.

I'm tired, I say.
I'm gonna take a nap.

Mom says okay,
hugs me gently
then lets me go
as tears well up
in her eyes.

> *But when you're ready, sweetie,*
> *there are some things*
> *we should talk about.*

And for the first time
        in a long time
my mother lets me see
her cry.

I Sleep

for
      what feels like

days.

I wake and sleep
          and wake again
turn over
drift off.

Sleep
until the sun
goes down
      and rises once more.

Sleep

because the thought of doing
anything else
is
impossible.

At Some Point

I half wake
to Mom sitting
on the edge of my bed,

smoothing my hair.

All of a sudden
I am little again.

All of a sudden
Mom and I are lying
next to each other
like we used to
when I was young,
when our bodies
still fit together.

She starts to hum.
   I am pulled
back into sleep.

When I Wake Again

it's dark out.

I look out my curtains

at the wedge of moon.

5:03 A.M., the clock says.

Now

I'm wide awake.

Now

I remember everything.

Now

my head hurts.

I just want to drift back

into oblivion.

Only now

I can't.

I Lie There

turn over and over in bed
      arm and head throbbing

dreading whatever comes next,
the conversations to come
          the questions
my forced exposure.

We talk
    and then what?

They make me stop?
They make me eat?
They make me give up my self-control?
        Lose everything
        I've worked for
and start all over
again?

        I can't.
This
is all I have.
    I can't get soft again
        weak again.
    I can't stay still
        stay here.

I have no other choice—

at 6:00 A.M.
I get up
pull on my coat
step into my boots

silently slip
      out the front door
into the still-dark morning.

It's Not Until

I get to the garage
that I realize:

      1. I can't ride with my arm in a cast.

      2. My bike is long gone.

I start walking.

The Cold Air

feels good on my face.

I have no plan
but I know I need
somewhere to go
where they can't find me
       can't make me
             give up everything
             I've worked so hard for.

Anna and I are still not talking.
Sky wouldn't get it.

So I make turns at random

     left
     right
     left again

until I have no idea
where I am.

I have
no one
to go to.

Nowhere
to go.

Dead ends
everywhere
I turn.

Twenty Minutes Later

I take a left
and recognize it:

the grassy parking strip
the red house with a wraparound porch
the rusty yellow fire hydrant

a few drops
of my own dried blood
painted on the sidewalk.

Everything
except
my bike.

A Lump Rises

in my throat.
I sit down
on the concrete.

My eyes well up.

Four days into the new year
I am
    alone
    shivering
with stitches in my skin
        dull pounding in my head
        a cast on my arm
        raw hunger in my stomach
            no scholarship
            no bike
            no best friend
and nowhere
that feels like
home.

I Picture

the people I love,
where they must be right now.

Anna
sleeping off a night of drinking
with her new friends,
mascara smudged on her smooth cheeks,
sparkles still on her eyelids.

Sky
in his messy, cozy apartment
soon to wake to coffee
and another day at the bustling restaurant.

Dad with his new love
in his new apartment
surrounded by new smiles.

And Mom,
who doesn't know I've run away
just so I don't have to face her.

Mom,
who has spent the past few months
living behind her bedroom door.

Mom,
who still remembers how to
braid my hair on the couch.

Mom,
who used to paint
and smile
and leave notes on my pillow.

Mom,
who is now at home alone,
unaware that I've left her
just like everyone else.

I Drag

a rock
along the sidewalk.

Scrape
scrape
scrape.

Toss it into the street.

Again.

Scrape
scrape
toss.

Scrape
scrape
toss.

My eye catches
on something green.

Hidden
out of sight
under the porch
of the house.

Its sleek metal body
starts to gleam
in the first light
of morning.

I run over
and hug my bike
with my one working arm.

Then I turn
and give in
to what I know
is my only option.

I walk my bike
as slowly as I can
        to prolong the moment
when I'll have to face it all.

By the Time I Get Home

it's almost nine.
Mom's bathrobed body
is on the porch,
phone in hand
looking distraught

till she sees me coming up the block
and we hurry toward each other
and embrace.

I Go Upstairs

to take a shower.
Carefully wrap my cast
in a plastic bag
like the doctor showed me.
      Turn on the water a little too hot
let it run over my scalp
try to wash off
everything I've done.

I come downstairs in sweatpants,
      a towel draped over my shoulders.

Mom's made oatmeal;
      a steaming bowl sits waiting for me
on the kitchen table.

My instinct is to push it away.
      The hollowness in my stomach
      is so familiar
      it feels right.

But Mom stands behind me with a brush,
      gently combing through my tangled strands
and I feel some knot in me
      wanting desperately to come untied.

So I give in,
      let her brush my wet hair
      take sweet
          slow bites.

I Wish

we could sit in silence
like this forever,
        comfort each other with contact.

She clears her throat.
What's been going on, sweetheart?

And I feel the question
land inside me
someplace soft.

This time
the lump in my throat gets too big
to ignore.
        This time
I know the words will come.

I turn
        bury my face in her stomach.
She wraps her arms around me.

        If I tell you,
        will you listen?

Of course, honey,
        she says.
I don't quite believe her
                but I want to.

        With my face in her shirt,
        smearing snot and tears
        on the white cotton,
        I tell her

        everything.

She Absorbs

my tears,
my saliva,
my stuttered words
my hurried breath.
      The afternoons alone
      the constant biking
      the daily weigh-ins
      the blogs I can't stop reading
      the skipped homework assignments
      the competition I missed completely.
All the output
of this messed-up function.

      Oh, Ivy.
      Why didn't you tell me you've been struggling?

Because you don't listen,
I say.
Because you're not really here.

      Her hands stop
      rubbing my back.

      I know.

      I'm sorry.
      I've been having
      a really hard time lately.

Tell me.
Please,
I say.

And

finally
she does.

She Says

it's like the world
is coated in blue-purple film.
Like everything is there
                she can see it all
it's just not sharp or interesting.

She picks up the brush again,
even though my hair's
all combed through.

> *I've struggled with depression*
> *   on and off*
> *since I was young,*
> *but with this transition,*
> *   me and your dad*
> *   and all,*
> *things have been harder than usual.*

I nod,
stir the oats slowly.

I just . . . I just feel like you left,
and you didn't tell me where you were going
or when you were coming back.

*   Oh, honey,*
she says.
*   I'm here.*

She says,
>Don't worry about me

and
>I'm getting help

and
>I'll be okay.
>I'm on new meds now
>and I'm starting to feel a little better.

More words I want to believe
but
I'm not sure I can.

So I Think

about numbers instead.

52: how old she is

15: how old I am

9: months she carried me in her belly

3: letters in my name, for the girl she desperately wanted

2: people it takes to fill our house now

1: mother who is working her way back

∞: the amount I know she loves me.

Mom Pours Us

both coffee.
We sit across
from each other.
        I stare down into my mug,
blow on the hot surface.

        I was so scared this morning, she says.

Me too, I say. *I'm sorry.*

        She sighs.
        *The doctor said you're at risk
        of an eating disorder.
        Your iron and blood pressure
        are really low.*

I look away.
It's not my fault.

        No one's saying that it is.
        She rushes to put her hands on mine.
        I pull them away.

I have it under control,
I say.
Can't meet her eyes.

        Okay, she says.

        *But they gave me the name of this doctor,
        a therapist.
        I'd like you to go.*

I don't need a therapist. I'm fine.

        *It's not a question, Iv.
        I made you an appointment this afternoon.*

Mom Drives Me

to Dr. Clarke's office
in a little brick building
nearby.

I don't need this,
I tell her in the car.
I told you—

> *I know, you think
> you have everything under control.*

She breathes in
like she's about to say more,
then stops.

What?

> *Listen,* she says. *This isn't really something I talk about.
> But I've struggled with this too.
> When I was younger, I . . .*
> She sighs.
> *I know what it's like.*
>
> *And trust me,
> this isn't something you can control on your own.*

She Says

the thoughts
can stay with you
forever
>the rules
>the games
>the fear
>the limits

the picking apart
of your body
in every mirror

>the fatigue
>the thrown-out lunches
>the avoidance.

She says depression
has made her own
issues worse.

She says
it can be
a lifelong war.

I turn toward the window.

I don't want this
to be the war
of my life.

I don't want this
to be
my story.

Mom's Words

play on a loop
in my head
as I walk in to see
Dr. Clarke,
        a serious, dark-haired woman
        in a book-lined office.

We talk about
a lot of
different things.
        School
        math
        Smart Girl
        my family
        Anna
        biking
        food
        and all the ways
        I keep my body
        in control.

That must be exhausting,
feeling like you need to be
in control every minute of every day.

        Yeah,
        I say.

        But it's worth it.

Is it?

I pause.

        Yeah.
        I think so.

Why?

> *Because if I'm not in control*
> *no one else will be.*
> The lump begins to rise.

She asks about
> the divorce.

> *It's fine,* I say.
> *It sucked.*
> *I got over it.*

She looks at me
softly.

You know, Ivy,
you don't have to be "over it."

> *Yeah, I do,* I say,
> but it's hard to speak
> because I'm crying.

You Know,

she says
after a long pause,
it's okay to grieve.

I pick at the fluffy gray fabric
of the pillow next to me.

When we lose something that's important to us,
we need to go through
a mourning period.

      It's not like anyone died, I say.

Maybe not.
But you lost something.

I feel a jerk
in my chest.

      Yeah,
      I say,
      that's true,

      and feel
      just a tiny bit
      lighter
      to admit it
      out loud.

How about this—
Dr. Clarke says
—just for tomorrow,
I'd like you to try to
give up some of your control.

Just a little bit.
Do you think you can do that?

   I really don't know.

But I say,
   I can try.

I Get Back

in the car
an hour later.

      Well?
Mom asks.

It was okay, I say.
She's not terrible.

Mom smiles
     pulls out of the lot.
We drive home
just as the sun is beginning to set
behind the evening's pink clouds.

The sky begins to drizzle,
a tiny
   light splattering.
I open the passenger-side window,
stick my hand out
to catch it.

Hey,

I say,
wanna drive to the beach?

      Mom makes a face. *It's January! It'll be freezing.*

I know.
But let's go anyway. Just to take a look.

      She gives me
      a small smile
      then agrees.

Twenty Minutes Later

we're at Matthews Beach,
the only car in the parking lot.

Let's go touch it, I say,
get out
run through the sand
toward the water's edge.

Mom walks behind.

I submerge my hands.
The water stings.

The sky is a blanket of gray
smudged pink at the horizon.
A lone seagull drifts by, squawking.

Mom dips in a pinky,
squeals, *It's so cold!*
She laughs,
and something in me
becomes buoyant.

For just a moment,
touching the water with me
on an afternoon in January
she feels delight in something.

And for a moment,
I do too.

Today

with its pink clouds
            clear water
talking with Mom and Dr. Clarke
        has been a soft escape.
        The release of a fist.

I think Mom
can feel it too.

I don't want
to leave,
step back into the daily life
                    of subtraction and silence
I've carved for myself.

Don't want the fist to clench again.
Don't want to feel its grip.

We Sit

side by side
in the sand.

I want to help you,
I say,
the back of my throat thick.
What can I do?

Mom shakes her head,
looks over at me.
Her eyes are desperate,
                        dark.

        There's nothing, she says.
        Just being here,
                being you.

She pulls me into
the space beside her,
and holds me while I sob.

We Get Back

in the car.
I look
at the evening sky
        the road signs boasting in big letters
all the places we could go.

        Mom, do you ever feel trapped? I ask.

She takes her eyes off the road
        turns to look at me
for just a second.

Not today,
she says.

        I nod.
        Not today.

Exponential Growth:

A model for growth of a quantity for which the rate
of growth is directly proportional to the amount present.
Growth whose rate becomes ever more rapid
in proportion to the growing total number or size.

The Few Days

before school starts again
are quiet.

I rarely leave the house.
Mom and I fall into
a slow rhythm,
a kind of peace.

We have our meals together
        for the first time in a while.
But it's hard to know
                how much to eat;
my wiring is all different now,
        signals crossed and confused
because of choices I made months ago.

Still
I try to let go of
some tiny slice
of self-control
        · try not to count bites
        try to listen to my body
        when it tells me I'm hungry or full.

On these mornings
when the gray of the sky feels impenetrable,
        Mom gets out her light box
        and we sit together
        in its glow.

The Last Day of Break

Mom takes me
to see a nutritionist,
a tall, smiling man
in an all-white office.

He tells me
I have anemia
     insufficient iron
to create
the red blood cells I need
to carry oxygen
so I can breathe
     think
     bike
     run
     walk
without getting out of breath
without having to stop.

He tells me
how many calories he wants me to eat
each day—
     it makes me sick.

I can't do that,
I tell him.
It's too much.

He looks at me,
concerned.
He doesn't know
about the locking door,
    the trap,
       the fist,
          the way
            this isn't
              a choice
                anymore.

We'll work up to it,
he says.

As if it were that easy.

But I Take

the brochures
the supplements
        home.

I read
the little numbers
on the side of the bottle.

Try to imagine
        filling myself
                my blood, my bones
                my inner tubes and vessels
        with iron and calcium—

good strong tools
to repair this
dysfunctional machine.

Before Mom Picks Me Up

I walk
to a nearby bookstore
leaf through an anatomy textbook.

I turn the pages with my good arm
pore over the pictures
of inside-out bodies
    thick muscles and ligaments.

This is my machine.

Made of a billion moving parts.
A feat of engineering,
working every second
to keep me alive.

When I get home later
       I take my schoolwork out,
finish the rest of
my missed assignments,
prepare myself
to start the year off right.

Monday Morning

brings me back to the city bus
                    the intersection
                    the circle of kids smoking on the corner
all of us wearing
heavy backpacks
      under a
heavier sky.

But I feel
      a bit lighter too.

Ella's in my ears again,
      carrying me toward school
ready
      to finish what I started.

I Don't Hear About It

until after second period.

A girl named Audrey comes up to my locker.
  Is Anna okay? I heard about what happened.
My stomach drops.
What do you mean?

Alcohol—
  too much.
Throwing up on the living room rug
then passing out.
Someone calling 911.
Hospital.
Stomach pumped.

Anna's small body
  with a tube in her throat
everything she ate and drank
pulled back up
the way it came.

It sounds
a bit too
  eerily
familiar.

I Picture

both of us
in the back
of screaming ambulances

in tacit agreement
not to reveal
the battles we fight
against our bodies.

Both of us
forced
to come clean.

Two silent girls
in hospital beds
wondering how the hell
we got here.

When the Bell Rings

for lunch
I'm relieved to see Anna
putting books away in her locker.

I take a deep breath,
      walk slowly up to her.
Hey.

She turns to me, wide-eyed.
      Did you hear?

Yeah.
We stand there
      awkward
      uncertain
for a moment.
Then I squeeze her hand.
She tenses
      then gives in.
Arms hanging limply at her sides,
      she leans over
presses her face
into my shoulder.

      I'm so embarrassed. Everyone knows.

It's okay, I say,
      the only thing I can think of.
It'll be okay.

She looks up, her face changing.
      Your shoulder is so bony, Iv.

It's Exactly

what I've been working for
what I've been wanting to hear.

But the way Anna says it
    with no bite,
    no jealousy,
    just wide eyes
    and soft voice,
it doesn't feel
like such a good thing.

We Walk

toward the cafeteria
slowly,
stepping gingerly
like this moment is fragile.

Tell me what happened,
I say.

They were playing beer pong
            and she was winning
and she was loving it
and I can picture her
laughing in her sequined top
feeling like a disco ball
like the most beautiful girl in the room

            and she doesn't know when it all started to spin
                and when drinking became
                    so much easier than talking
            and when it got hard to walk straight
            and when she began to get nauseous
            and couldn't find Raquel
            or her phone
                until she woke up in the hospital.

Okay, your turn, she says.
And don't leave anything out.

We Stop

in a hallway
cleared of students.

       At first
I try
       to pick
my words
       as sparingly
as I pick
       my bites

weighing
       what I can
reveal

but pretty soon
       it's all spilling out of me
       there is no control
just tears
       as I tell Anna everything:

my restrictions
       my body
my mom
my fall
       the missed competition
the miles and miles of biking
       the afternoons
when all I can do is
       sleep
my plan to try
       to get back on track.

I am a faucet
       that cannot be turned off
and Anna
takes in everything
       that pours out of me.

She Asks,

Why didn't you tell me any of this before?

>   *You were gone, I say, half accusing*
>
>   *half apologizing.*
>   *This whole summer.*
>   *This whole fall.*
>   *I needed you, and you were gone.*

Her eyes are even wider now,
a tear falls from each one as she blinks.

I know.

I'm sorry.

But you were too, Ivy.

She Hugs Me

and in that moment
my body
doesn't feel like
        enemy
        or cage
        or machine
    but a vessel
through which we can touch.

I hug her back,
hard.

Even though it traps me,
even though I can't escape this sheath of tight skin,
I can use it
for a few seconds
    to show Anna
        that I love her
        that I'm sorry
        too.

We Find a Spot

to eat on the stairwell.
Anna texts Raquel
      asks if she and I
      can have lunch alone.

I take out a bag of baby carrots.

I can feel Anna's eyes on me,
how she watches as I bring
each one to my mouth,
how she looks away
      hesitates
looks back again.

I'm glad you're trying,
she says,
to get better.

      Thanks,
      I say,
      even though it's hard.

      How'd the soccer season finish up?

She launches into
the story of her best goal,
      the finals,
         the girls picked to be next year's captains.

I sit back and slowly crunch,
listen to the familiar music of my best friend's voice
      the rhythms of her hand gestures
      better than
      all the jazz standards
      in the world.

She signs
my cast

    Sisters Forever
    xoxo
    Anna

and as we sit there
talking,
I feel the ground beneath us
shift.

The Bell Rings

my stomach drops.

Calculus.
Ms. Fulton.

I take a deep breath
  walk inside.

She sees me and gasps.
        Ivy! What happened to your arm?

I couldn't make it. To the competition.
I'm sorry.
I look at the gray-green carpet.

        Oh. Well—

I know I let you down.

Finally,
I meet her eyes.

I really wanted to be there.
I was on my way . . .
Things have just been really hard.

        She squeezes my shoulder,
        says,
        I'm very sorry to hear that.
        Trust me, though.
        You haven't let anybody down.

But the scholarship.
I need it.

        I understand.

But try not to put too much pressure on yourself.
Math is something you love, right?

Yeah.

How about we keep it that way?

I smile.

After School

on Friday
Mom drives me
to Dr. Clarke's again.

We talk more about
      how I've been doing with food
          relaxing some control
      what I see when I look in the mirror
      all the pressure I put on myself.

She says whenever I get overwhelmed
      thoughts racing
         heart pumping
            panic rising
               fist clenching
                  nails digging

I can just focus on my breath.

    Inhale, exhale.
    Inhale, exhale.
    Inhale, exhale.

Notice what's happening in your mind,
she says.
You can always choose to let a thought go,
               to just count your breaths.
Just think about getting from
one breath to the next.
No matter what. Okay?

    Inhale, exhale.

    Okay.

I Leave

her office
walk out into the parking lot
where the cold winter light
      bounces off car windows.

Mom is waiting for me
in the driver's seat,
      sunglasses and
      heat on.

I watch her sit there with a half smile
her face turned up toward the sky.

She is a desert plant,
drinking the light of the sun
through a straw.
Huddling
by the artificially heated air,
out of her natural habitat.

You should move back to Arizona someday,
I tell her
as I slide into
the passenger seat.

      She laughs.
      Maybe someday
      I will.

At Home

I practice counting breaths

practice recharging
my body
my machine.

In, out.
        One.
In, out.
        Two.

Clean air swirling
through my pipes.

*Healthier input
equals healthier output.*

With my finger

on my inner wrist

I trace letters that say:

        just breathe.

Permission

to let go of everything else

for just
        one
                second.

Anna Comes Over

for a sleepover,
the first one in months.

She joins me and Mom on the couch.
We fall
into this moment together
so easily:
my legs across Anna's,
my head on Mom's shoulder.

We watch a *Dancing with the Stars* marathon,
make fun of the celebrities,
pick our favorite routines.

When Anna giggles,
I can feel her body shake,
the vibrations transmitted through my calves.
Mom lifts her small fingers,
    combs them through my hair.

The three of us form an unbroken chain.
The line of our bodies is a live wire.

We watch the dancers
    twirl
    kick
    sashay around the dance floor
and I'm warmed
    by this sudden sense of connectedness
    our physical selves in simple contact
this returning to an old, forgotten place,
        somewhere you used to love,
        buried deep inside your memory.

    Like when you walk in the door
    and say
    Oh, this is home.

So Maybe

home is something
      that changes as we do,
something that expands and contracts
      with time and loss.

This house has not felt like home in months;
      the roof I no longer visit,
the rooms uninhabited.

But right now,
with my head resting
      in the nook of Mom's neck
      Anna by my side
our bodies melting together
this I know
is home.

Anna Goes

to the kitchen
        makes us some popcorn
        brings a huge bowl back with a smile.

It's delicious,
warm, salty.
Stopstopstop.

It's hard to turn off the part of my brain
that counts each piece I allow in,
that knows the amount of calories in each cup of popcorn
            the numbers I've committed to memory.

But I tell these thoughts to go away
                    like Dr. Clarke said.
I notice them,
but try not to follow what they say.

        Inhale, exhale. One.

        Inhale, exhale. Two.

        Inhale, exhale. Three.

They get quieter
        recede
        shrink.

        Inhale, exhale. Four.

I Lie Awake

feeling my stomach,
the slight bloat from the salt.

I feel the familiar panic rising.
A clenching of my stomach
a tightness in my chest.

       Inhale, exhale. One.

Anna's deep-breathing body
sound asleep on my floor,
blond curls spread on the pillow,
a gentle snore every few minutes.

I take deep
slow breaths.
Try to let go of every other thought.

I look up at the half moon.

Maybe.

Maybe I can just
      get through tonight
and maybe for now
that is something.

Maybe I can walk,
slowly,
out of this.

A tiptoe
      maybe
toward something better.

In the Morning

winter sun streams in through the windows.

We drop Anna off
stop at Mom's favorite coffee shop
        a cozy spot on the hill.
Sit at the window table,
        sipping warm drinks,
        sifting through the gray sky
        for any patches of blue.

You know, she tells me,
I'm really proud of you.

                You are?
                Why?

Because you're trying.
Because you're you.
Because I love you no matter what.

        And I feel a different kind of sunburst
        shine within me,
        a softer, warmer one—
                so different from how I feel
                when I look in the mirror
                or step on the scale,
                things that make me feel like
                I am on the way to being enough—
        because Mom's words,
        and the way we face the sky together,
        eyes pointed toward the light,
        hands warmed by steaming mugs,
        these things make me feel like

        maybe

        I already am.

Like maybe
there's a light.

Like maybe Mom
can feel it too.

I've Always Known

that Mom was desperate
                    for a girl

and I was proud
that I could fill some hole inside her.

But now I have my own holes to fill
                    my own work to do.

Maybe I
can be the one
to break this line of heavy inheritance,
            this chain
                    of hunger.

I Wake Early

the first day of February,
look out my window
see a rare flurry of snow.

Something else is different too:
Mom's studio.
The lights are on.

An orange glow comes
from inside,
a small puff of smoke
from the chimney.
Movement passes
back and forth
behind the windows.

A sign of life
after so many
quiet years.

I Get Up

put on slippers and a sweater
walk through the cold air
knock lightly.

No answer.

I open the door.

Her back is to me
      she's lost in concentration.

A small fire burns
in the hearth my dad built years ago.
Quiet music fills the room.

Then I see what she's painting.

A thin face
with large green eyes.
A crop of brown hair, gray at the roots,
lying in waves to the chin.
Wrinkles in the forehead from a long and twisting life,
      years of laughter and worry.

The eyes are unmistakable
staring back at me
      at the warm room
      at this February morning
at us trying our hardest
always trying.

Reaching for each other,
missing,
but reaching again
      and again.

I can't take my eyes off the picture.
It's too beautiful.

Here in this room
filled with goddesses,

my mother is painting
herself.

I Tiptoe Back

to the kitchen
not wanting to disturb her
         to tell her
how good it feels
to see her painting
again.

The hearth glows in my chest.
I warm the kettle for coffee,
take my iron supplement,
stretch,
lean over,
touch my toes.

The simple movement of my body
feels so good.

The stretch.
The warmth of fire on the skin.
The weaving of fingers through the hair.
Even the cold floor beneath bare feet.

I had forgotten
all the things
a body can feel.

I will try,
I tell myself.
I will try to remember.

Acknowledgments

Thank you to Liza Kaplan Montanino for working so closely with me to bring this book to life. Your inspired ideas and expert advice allowed Ivy to tell her story, and I am so grateful. Thank you also to Michael Green, Talia Benamy, and everyone at Philomel for making this book a reality. Thank you to Erin Murphy for your support, advice, and belief in me.

Thank you to Kate Weiner and Betsy Rapoport for reading an early draft, for giving me so much wisdom, and for being two of the most amazing women I've ever met. I'm honored to know you both.

Thank you to Lucy Cheadle for being my expert calculus consultant, and for being one of the most badass women alive. So grateful for your friendship since day one.

Thank you to Daniel Pope for reading sections and for stubbornly encouraging me to believe that I could do this.

Thank you to the WeSlam and Writers' Bloc communities at Wesleyan for giving me a home. So many of you have touched me, inspired me, changed me. Thank you to Button Poetry for the platform you give to spoken-word poets.

Thank you to my sisters in writing and art, who've given me support, inspiration, ferocity, joy, and friendship: Alison Znamierowski, Kate Gibbel, Chelsea Coreen, Caroline Rothstein, Raechel Rosen, Cherkira Lashley, Caroline Catlin, Emily Weitzman, all of The Coven, and so many more.

Jonas and Isaac, you are the best brothers a girl could ever ask for. Thanks, Jo, for the jazz recommendations. Mom and Dad, thanks for loving me unconditionally, for supporting me always, and for making me believe I am capable of anything. I love you.

Additional Resources

If you struggle with disordered eating or body-image obsession, you are not alone. By speaking openly and supporting one another, we can heal from the internalized, destructive pressure to control and shrink our bodies. It's a devastating battle to try to fight alone. Below is a list of resources that can help provide support.

Websites and Blogs with Body-Positive/Self-Love Content:
- The Body Is Not an Apology: thebodyisnotanapology.com
- HelloFlo: helloflo.com
- Proud2BMe: proud2bme.org
- Intuitive Eating: intuitiveeating.com
- Caroline Rothstein: www.carolinerothstein.com
    (Also check out Caroline's Body Empowerment series on YouTube!)
- Jenni Schaefer: www.jennischaefer.com
- Virgie Tovar: www.virgietovar.com
- June Alexander www.junealexander.com

Prevention and Recovery Organizations:
- NEDA: www.nationaleatingdisorders.org
- The Elisa Project: theelisaproject.org
    (*Additional Treatment Information* page under the *Resources* menu)
- Mental Fitness, Inc.: mentalfitnessinc.org
- Eating Disorders Coalition: www.eatingdisorderscoalition.org
- National Association of Anorexia Nervosa and Associated Disorders: www.anad.org
- Binge Eating Disorder Association: bedaonline.com
- Alliance for Eating Disorders: www.allianceforeatingdisorders.com
- Trans Folx Fighting Eating Disorders: www.transfolxfightingeds.org

Supplemental Reading:
- *When Food Is Love: Exploring the Relationship Between Eating and Intimacy*, by Geneen Roth.
- *Intuitive Eating: A Revolutionary Program That Works (3rd Edition)*, by Evelyn Tribole and Elyse Resch.
- *Using Writing as a Therapy for Eating Disorders: The Diary Healer*, by June Alexander.

Treatment Centers:
- BALANCE Eating Disorder Treatment Center (New York, NY)
- Oliver-Pyatt Centers (Miami, FL)
- Monte Nido (various locations across the country)
- Veritas Collaborative (Durham, NC; Richmond, VA; Atlanta, GA)